LAST MAN IN LAZARUS

When a town marshal is murdered by five escaping prisoners and his new bride is abducted, the killers think they have avoided the justice they deserve. But the dead man's older brother is Nathan Holly, a feared and relentless US marshal who is more than happy to take up the pursuit. Holly rides north with a Paiute tracker, Tukwa — a man conducting his own quest for vengeance. Both will end their search amidst the winter snows of a mining town called Lazarus . . .

Books by Bill Shields
in the Linford Western Library:

THE SNAKE RIVER BOUNTY

WARS T₆

BILL SHIELDS

LAST MAN IN LAZARUS

Complete and Unabridged

LINFORD
Leicester

First published in Great Britain in 2012 by
Robert Hale Limited
London

First Linford Edition
published 2013
by arrangement with
Robert Hale Limited
London

A catalogue record for this book is available
from the British Library.

ISBN 978–1–4448–1132–2

Published by
F. A. Thorpe (Publishing)
Anstey, Leicestershire

Set by Words & Graphics Ltd.
Anstey, Leicestershire
Printed and bound in Great Britain by
T. J. International Ltd., Padstow, Cornwall

This book is printed on acid-free paper

1

The Night Camp

Snow fell in lazy spirals out of a leaden sky. Darkness wasn't far off as Nathan Holly sniffed the air. The smell of a wood fire carried a long way on the cold, windless mountain air, and Holly had followed it for the last two miles. This close he felt like sparks were pricking at his nostrils. He studied the tracks he'd just crossed. The dirty, churned-up snow told its story of a heavily laden wagon, one riderless horse and three mounted men.

The wagon was unexpected. The three riders were not. He'd been hunting them since the last week in September and it was now early November. Was this a rendezvous with other members of the gang? Why here? And what was a wagon doing up here in

1

the hills? If they were heading into Logan the trail was quite a ways back.

Holly dismounted, slid his Winchester rifle out of its saddle holster, checked the load and then did the same for his two revolvers. He tethered the pinto to a tree branch and climbed a sharp incline, careful of the treacherous snow and the slick of ice that covered exposed rock. There was a natural game trail down below, twisting between rocky outcroppings and snow-heavy ponderosa pine. The wagon had come up that way, but Holly wanted a close look at their night camp before riding in. He didn't reckon on being surprised.

The glow of a fire showed in the darkening sky above a high ledge of rock. He could hear its snap and spit. Holly got down on his belly and inched forward. The scent of burning wood mingled with the warm smell of freshly made coffee. He could hear voices now: rough male laughter and a woman telling someone called Johnny to get to bed, followed by a young boy's protests. The woman sounded desperate, and worried about something more than the boy getting his rest.

Holly peered over the rock edge in time to see a boy of about twelve climbing over an open tailgate into a covered wagon. There was a shotgun visible, resting just inside the open flaps. The man seated closest to it kept shooting nervous glances at the weapon, as if wishing it closer. He was a stocky young man with a blunt, honest face and clear blue eyes that flitted from the shotgun to the three other men seated opposite him, on the other side of the campfire. The woman was obviously his companion, probably his wife. She sat close beside him, using his stocky body to shield herself from view of the other men. She had a plain but determined-looking face. Her lips were pressed together in a tight line of tension.

That the cause of her anxiety was the three men, Holly did not doubt. One was a big beefy man with a thick black beard only a little darker than his close-set eyes. He wore a wide-brimmed black hat and a black fur coat spacious enough for even his excessive bulk. Beside him a smaller, much wirier man lay propped up on one elbow. He had a gunpowder burn on his left cheek and watchful eyes that rarely shifted from their contemplation of the woman. The third man sat a little ways off, just out of the flickering circle of firelight, his back to Holly. He wore a yellow slicker and held a rifle across his knees. Cigar smoke curled up around his hat brim, its unusually pungent odour drifting up to where Holly lay. His attention was fixed on the couple by the wagon. He was waiting for the man to make a wrong move towards the shotgun.

There were seven horses tethered close to the wagon, six to pull the heavily-laden wagon and a seventh spare in case they lost one, or in the event someone needed to ride out alone, for supplies or for help, or perhaps just to scout the terrain up ahead. Three horses belonging to Black Beard and his friends were tethered to branches on the far side of the campfire, close to where Yellow Slicker sat.

Black Beard and Powder Burn were telling the woman what good coffee she made, but the smirking glances they exchanged made their intentions clear enough. They were working up to more than just intentions and the husband, if such he was, knew that time was running out fast. He would never reach the shotgun before the man with the rifle shot him down, but Holly figured he would probably make a try for it. He eased back from the rock edge and got himself back down the incline.

Before mounting the pinto he unfastened his thigh-length sheepskin coat and left it open. The frosty air crept under it, chasing the warmth and chilling him instantly. Better to be cold, he reasoned, than unable to reach his guns, especially since he'd decided to just ride on in and give these people a hand. Pulling his battered white Stetson down to cover his eyes, he urged the pinto forwards. The silence of the winter night was broken by the crisp scrunch of hoofs on freshly fallen snow.

As he got close he called out, 'Hello the camp!'

There was no immediate answer, just startled voices that conferred with each other in hasty, hushed tones.

'Thought I might warm myself by your fire, maybe have a cup of coffee if you're agreeable?'

'Sure. Come on in,' someone barked back.

Black Beard and Powder Burn greeted his approach with watchful eyes and uneasy silence. Yellow Slicker had drifted into the tree line behind him. A dusting of snow from disturbed branches betrayed his position over on Holly's left flank, about thirty paces away. The clean scent of spruce was fouled with the unappealing scents of cigar smoke, unwashed clothing and skin.

'I'm sure happy to see you folks,' Holly told them as he dismounted. 'I got off the trail somewhere and I reckon I'm about as lost as I've ever been. I was frozen solid to this here saddle before I caught scent of your coffee. Had me a thought to thaw out some, maybe find out where in this frozen hell I am.'

He caught the relieved look the woman exchanged with her man. The thought was as plain as if she'd spoken it. He wasn't with these men, and his presence might make them reconsider whatever they'd been about to do. She followed the look with a worried glance at the wagon. As he tethered his pinto to the tailgate Holly followed her glance with a questioning look.

'Our son is asleep in there,' she said. 'The climb has him all tuckered out.'

'Can't say as I blame him,' the father added, with a meaningful look towards the two men seated on the far side of the fire. 'We were told there was a trail through these hills would get us into town a mite faster than going around. I guess someone was misinformed.'

7

Holly stepped over to the fire but didn't sit. 'I like my coffee real hot,' he said to the woman. 'Hot enough to take skin off,' he added.

As she poured and then handed him a steaming mug, he said, 'You mean you folks are as lost as I am? Well then, I guess I don't feel so foolish after all. Who are you, if you don't mind my asking?'

'My name is Harvey Norton, and this is my wife, Rachel. Our son, Johnny, is asleep in the wagon.' This last bit of information was inaccurate. Holly could hear a soft rustling that meant young Johnny was awake and taking an interest. He hoped the boy would stay put when the shooting started, as it most assuredly would once the niceties were over. The tension was like a strung wire about to snap.

'We're bound for a stop-over in Logan,' Norton continued, 'before heading up north. There's a silver town up there on the Marys River and we're aiming to start up a general store. We got the initial stock in the wagon and we're hoping to buy more in Logan, and then get it sent on to us in a day or two. There's a feller called Tom Loomis is supposed to meet us in town.'

'A silver town, north of Logan?' Holly was puzzled. 'There used to be a mine called the 'Crazy Mike'. It was worked by a fellow called Crazy Mike Barton, but it was all played out before any town got built. Last I heard there were a few shacks left standing, but not much else.'

'It seems that Barton pulled out too soon,' Norton told him. 'He sold what he believed to be a played out mine to a man called Lester Ryle. Ryle had a geologist do a proper survey. He found a much bigger lode and got the men and equipment in to mine it properly. He renamed the mine and the town that's sprung up around it. Brought it back from the dead and called it Lazarus: I guess Mr Ryle has a sense of humour. It's a proper boom town now.'

All the time Harvey Norton had been

talking, Holly had been watching the other two men. He'd moved, slow and careful, sniffing at the scalding coffee which was too hot to drink, so as to place Black Beard, Powder Burn and their mounts between him and the hidden rifleman. A soft whisper of falling snow gave the man away every time he moved, most likely trying to keep the new arrival covered.

'So how did you end up lost?' Holly asked. 'The trail into Logan is clear enough marked.'

Norton threw a cautious look at Black Beard. 'We met up with these gentlemen around noon. They told us they knew about a pass through the hills. With the snow coming we figured on getting into town a mite faster.'

They brought you up here to kill and rob you, Holly thought, away from any possible witnesses or interference from others who might happen along the trail.

Black Beard was tiring of the conversation between Holly and Norton. 'Who are you anyways, mister?' His voice was an ugly bark. 'What you doin' ridin' alone in these hills? In this damned weather as well? If the trail into Logan is so clear how come you got so lost?'

As he spoke Black Beard sized the stranger up. What he saw he didn't take to. The man was tall, broad in the shoulders and with a strong, unhandsome face. He had a large nose that seemed a perfect fit for a big rough face that looked carved out of solid granite. The set of the mouth was grimly determined, showing the nature of a man who could and would impose his will if he thought it necessary. But it was the eyes that disturbed the most — cold blue chips of ice that settled on a man like judgement come a'calling.

He also had way too many guns for comfort: a Colt single-action Army revolver holstered on his right side; the heavier Colt model 1851 Navy revolver hung on the left, the handle facing inwards for a fast cross-draw; leather pockets looped along the gunbelt

11

carried extra ammunition. Whoever he was, his armaments were serious business: he looked like he could fight a war all by himself.

'I guess I'm heading north as well,' Holly replied mildly.

'North — that covers a lot of territory.'

'I reckon it does.'

Rachel Norton said quickly, 'Perhaps you could ride with us.'

Black Beard scowled. 'I'm a mite fussy about who I share the trail with. I asked you a question, mister — who are you and what are you doing up here?'

Holly smiled, but there was no humour in it. He talked slowly, taking his time. 'There was a killing in a little town called Creevy up in Oregon a few weeks back. Maybe you heard about it. There was a ruckus in the town's saloon and the owner, a man called Lomas Conway, had the man who started it thrown out into the street. The man was a drifter with a reputation for trouble. I guess that drifter felt some resentment towards Conway, because him and two of his drifter friends did some skulking outside in a dark alley. When Conway stepped out sometime later that night, they gunned him down. Didn't give him a chance, just started blasting away from the cover of that alley. Then they lit out like the low murdering cowards they were.'

Black Beard tensed, his hand creeping towards his sidearm. Powder Burn eased up off his elbow, sat upright, his posture no longer relaxed. They were both ready to pull on the tall stranger. The moment was close and Rachel Norton moved aside as her husband caught Holly's eye and flicked a meaningful glance towards the rifleman's position in the trees. Holly gave a brief nod of understanding.

Black Beard wasn't done talking. As he got to his feet he said, 'Well now, that's one hell of a tragic story you got there, but it don't answer my questions. I already asked twice who you are and what you're doin' up here.'

Holly took a few steps towards the man before replying. 'I'm a United States marshal and I'm tracking the killers of Lomas Conway. They came over into Nevada and last I heard they'd crossed the Humboldt and were headed towards Logan. Maybe you came across them. One's called Dan Morrow and has a thick black beard, one's a skinny runt with a powder burn on his face, called Deeley Watts, and one wears a yellow slicker. The only name I have for him is Teague, and the information that he smokes a particular sort of cheap Mexican cigar that smells of pig droppings.'

Black Beard swallowed hard. 'And what's your name, mister?'

The snow was falling much thicker now, a curtain that hid everything outside the circle of firelight. The sizzle of snowflakes melting in the campfire's heat could be clearly heard in the seconds before the tall stranger replied, 'Nathan Holly.'

The name was the trigger. It told

Black Beard and Powder Burn that there was but one chance for escape. They went for their guns.

Holly threw the scalding coffee in Black Beard's face in the same second he pulled his Colt single-action and put two slugs into Powder Burn as he tried to rise. Black Beard screamed in pain and staggered backwards, one hand at his face and the other clawing his handgun clear of the holster. He never got a shot off. As he stumbled into Yellow Slicker's line of fire his body jerked with the impact of rifle bullets meant for Holly.

Holly dropped to the ground in the same moment as Black Beard fell dying. He aimed at Yellow Slicker's position, hoping to get him before the rifle-man had a chance to move, but an explosion from behind blasted the branches apart and sent a thick cloud of snow swirling around on the frozen air. Norton rushed forward with the shot-gun aimed, ready to unload the second barrel, but the snow cloud was thick enough to hide the rifleman if he was still a threat. Holly yelled for him to get down.

Seconds passed as the last echo of gunfire died away, leaving only the dying gasps of Black Beard and the terrified yells of the boy in the wagon. Rachel Norton climbed in beside him, trying to quiet him down. She knew that the marshal and her husband needed silence. As the boy's yells became muffled sobs, Holly and Norton listened and watched.

'You think he's dead?' Norton whispered at length. It had been all of two minutes without a sound or movement from within the tree line. Black Beard had quit his dying gasps and lay still, finally expired.

Before Holly could reply the sharp cracking of a tree branch broke the silence. It sounded quite a ways in and there was no way to know if it was mule deer or antelope or prowling bobcat, or maybe a wounded man making his escape.

Holly sighed. 'If it's Teague I can't leave him wandering around out there.

He might come at us again when we ain't expecting him.'

Norton looked at the dense, snow-laden tree line, in which a man could lie low and bushwhack anyone foolish enough to try for him. The snow was falling thicker than ever, a moving curtain that brought visibility down to only a few feet in any direction.

'You're not going in there?'

'I got no choice. Take care of your family and keep a sharp eye. Stay out of the firelight.'

As Norton reloaded the shotgun and eased back into the shadows, Holly slid his Winchester from its saddle holster and vanished into the heavy snowfall.

2

Blood on the Snow

That Norton's shotgun blast had done some damage wasn't in doubt. Blood splatter on the snow, and around the shattered tree branches that had sheltered the rifleman, told their story of a badly injured man. The question was how bad — bad enough to be dying, or just bad enough to be lying up somewhere, waiting for some poor fool to come looking?

Holly moved slow and careful, following the blood trail but keeping off to the side of it, hugging the cover of shadows beneath snow-heavy branches. The deeper he penetrated into the darkened wood the harder it was to make out much of anything. Stark black twisting shadows and big fat drifting flakes, ghostly white and silent: that was all the world was to him. He wanted to slow up even more, but the snow was covering the blood trail far too quickly.

He stopped every few moments despite the fading trail, allowing his heart to slow down so it didn't thunder in his ears and drown the sounds around him. He listened to the soft fall of snow and the rustling feathers of some night bird out hunting prey, but there came no human sounds of a desperate and wounded man pushing through the wood.

After about ten minutes of this he came across the body. A clearing in the trees backed on to a rock face, about twenty feet high and too steep for an injured man to climb. Teague lay at the base, already half buried in the thickening snowfall. The yellow slicker and the hat showed through the fresh fall. Another few minutes he'd likely be covered up.

Holly started a cautious approach, taking dead aim with the Winchester. The half-buried body didn't stir at all, but Holly wasn't about to make any foolish assumptions. He was but five paces away when a random breeze carried the faint whiff of cheap cigar to his nostrils. It came, not from the supposed corpse, but from a position to his right, just inside the tree line. He dropped to the ground a second before the bark of a rifle sent a slug past his right ear. He felt the hot wind of its passing and sent an answering shot back in the same direction it had come from.

There was a crashing of tree branches as Holly levered another round into the Winchester and fired again, hitting the blood-soaked man who stumbled out of the trees. The bullet hit him in the face, punching his nose back into his skull.

Teague was probably dead before he hit the ground, but Holly wasn't about to take it on faith. This man had been hard enough to kill. He took his time in kicking the body over so it lay face up. What was left of the face wasn't for showing to the faint of heart.

Holly shot a rueful look at the slicker and hat, left as bait while Teague waited in the trees. The ambush had almost succeeded.

'Well, I reckon I done for you this time,' Holly said, 'unless you got some way of coming back from the dead.' He sniffed the air. 'Still smells like pig droppings.'

★ ★ ★

Holly got the family moving the following morning. They headed back down on to the main trail with Holly riding alongside the covered wagon. Harvey Norton was driving the team, his wife seated beside him. Young Johnny sat in the rear of the wagon, staring at the corpses, wrapped in saddle blankets and draped across the saddles of the three mounts tied to the tailgate.

'I saw when you dragged that last one in,' the boy chattered, his voice all rushed and excited and frightened at the same time. 'You shot his nose off,' he added, not quite accurately. 'There was just a bloody hole in the middle of his face.'

His mother turned and snapped, 'Johnny, you get away from there. Get up front here with us.' Concern was written plainly across her face. 'He never should have seen such a sight,' she added.

Holly reckoned the criticism was aimed his way, and he said, 'I surely do apologize, ma'am, but I couldn't leave the body lying out there.'

'You got nothing to apologize for,' Harvey said hastily, shooting a look at his wife. 'If you hadn't come along we were all likely dead.'

Young Johnny piped up from between his parents, 'What were they gonna do, if Mr Holly hadn't killed them? Would they have hurt you . . . and Ma?' His shocked voice showed his disbelief that anyone would intentionally mean his mother harm.

Harvey reached back and tousled his

straw-coloured hair, by way of reassurance. 'I reckon they might, son. The world is filled with no-good varmints what don't give a cuss who they hurt, so long as they gratify their appetites for money and violence.'

'Harvey — ' Rachel warned.

'He'll have to learn such unpleasant truths sometime,' Harvey shrugged. 'With what nearly happened last night, I reckon it's time.'

Between Harvey and his wife, Johnny's eyes were wide and round. 'Ma always said it weren't good to be hurting other folk. But I guess it was okay for you and Mr Holly to kill those men.'

'It had to be done and that's the painful truth,' Harvey told him. 'Sometimes you got to defend what's yours and the people you love.'

As the boy fell into a silent reflection on what his father had said, Holly asked, 'What made you leave the trail and follow those men?'

Harvey sighed. 'They rode up all friendly like, helpful as can be. Fool that I am I was tired and worried about the weather closing in on the open trail. They said they lived in Logan and were taking a short cut through the hills, where the trees would offer some shelter from the snow that was surely on the way. It was only after we left the main trail that I started to get nervous, but it was too late to turn back without them asking why I'd changed my mind. I figured telling them the truth would only make them mad, and maybe start whatever they had planned a mite early. I needed to get close to the shotgun, and not perched up on the wagon seat like a sitting target. Once we made camp they began working themselves up to doing what they'd brought us up there for. I was about to go for the shotgun when you rode in. I never would have made it, would I?'

Holly shook his head. 'Teague was just waiting for you to make your try.'

Seated beside her husband, Rachel Norton shuddered. Holly understood. Her imagination was playing out the scene after her husband had been killed. After a second her eyes flickered and fell on Holly, showing clearly her thanks that he'd come along.

She said, 'Those men knew your name. They went for their guns as soon as you told them who you were.'

'They knew me, sure enough,' Holly replied. 'There's hardly a troublemaking outlaw hardcase from Flagstaff to Frisco who don't know my name. I been marshalling for a good twenty years or more, and I'm still drawing breath. That kind of gets you a reputation, whether you want it or not. If you asked me personal, I could live without it. It makes my job harder when they know I'm coming.'

Harvey smiled. 'I have heard of you, Marshal. You're a bit of a legend, if you don't mind my saying. You have a brother, don't you, over by Stillwater?'

'That's right.' Guilt clouded Holly's eyes for a moment. 'He's the town marshal. He got himself hitched a few months back, and I'm ashamed to admit I didn't make the wedding. I ain't even seen the bride yet. But I'll make it one of these days.'

'Family are important, Mr Holly,' Rachel chided. 'Don't leave it so long that they become strangers.'

'No ma'am, I surely won't.'

They travelled in silence for a while. The day was crisp, and around noon the cloud cover broke and a weak sun was seen riding a cobalt-blue sky. Skinny black crows circled overhead in the vast emptiness, knowing that dead flesh lay bundled beneath the saddle blankets. Their cawing cries added a dismal accompaniment to the creak of wagon wheels and the rattle of saddle harness, and the snorts and whinnies of the horses.

At length Holly asked where the family had been settled, before the present trek to the silver town.

'We had us a store in Lincoln,' Harvey said, 'down in New Mexico territory. Ran a dry-goods store for a few years, before a man called L G

Murphy and his partner, James Dolan, decided they'd like a monopoly on dry goods in Lincoln County. Then one of the big ranchers figured Murphy was having it all his own way, and him and another rancher started their own store. Pretty soon we got squeezed out. I figured it was time to move anyways. There's big trouble brewing back there: gonna be a lot of people get hurt, you mark my words.'

'So how did you meet this Lester Ryle?'

'He came through Lincoln a few times. He seemed a right nice fellow, if a mite ambitious. The last time he came through he'd been buying up mining equipment. When he saw how things were going in Lincoln he made me an offer; said his new town needed a general store and he'd always liked my operation. So we sold out to the faction opposing Murphy, packed what we could, and headed for Nevada.'

'Well, I surely do wish you well,' Holly said. 'If I ever get up that way, I'll be sure and look you up, see what you've made of this new silver town.'

'We'll be right pleased to receive you, Marshal.' Rachel smiled. 'And I'm sorry I sounded so waspish earlier. I really do thank you for what you did.'

'Think nothing of it. Just doing my job, Mrs Norton, but I'm glad to have helped.'

Johnny Norton sat between his parents, all still and thoughtful. Holly caught him staring at the Winchester and smiled at him. Johnny smiled back, nervous and unsure, before he went back to staring at the rifle.

* * *

It was late afternoon when they got into Logan. The Norton family headed for the livery stable to get the wagon stowed and the horses cared for. They intended booking in at the town's only hotel until it was time to head on north. Harvey expected to meet up with Tom Loomis at the hotel.

Holly took the three horses and their burdens down to the town marshal's office. He'd been seen coming into town with the blanket wrapped corpses, and the marshal was waiting for him by the office door, a young deputy by his side. Holly knew the older man, recognized the tobacco stained white moustache and watchful eyes of Sam Sugar. Sugar had been a lawman for many years, in cow towns and boom towns and far too many trouble spots to bother counting.

'Well, hello there, Sugar, so this is where you're nesting nowadays.'

The absence of any returned salutation gave Holly pause. He looked more carefully at Sugar. The man's mouth was a thin line of tension and his eyes had none of their usual sparkle. Bad news was coming, that was for sure.

'What is it, Sam?'

Sugar started to speak, stopped and spat a long stream of tobacco juice on the ground, then tried again. 'Telegraph office got a message for you, should you

29

happen this way. Your brother, James — there was a jailbreak over in Stillwater. James got himself shot.'

Holly was unaccustomed to shivers of fear running down his spine, but he felt them now, cold as ice. 'Shot bad?' he asked, his voice coming out a frightened croak that those who knew him would never have recognized.

'He's dead, Nathan. He's been shot dead, and his wife is missing. They think the killers took her with them.'

3

The Missing and the Dead

The four men stood on a high rise of rocky ground, two of them on either side of a large flat slab of stone. Their attention was on its pitted surface and the blood, long dried into a dark brown stain. Nathan Holly's giant frame dwarfed the county sheriff, Leonard Tope, who appeared nervous, standing in the marshal's shadow. The other two stood a distance back, holding the horses and showing deference to the lawmen. One was a Paiute tracker called Tukwa, and the other a store-owner called Sefton; both had ridden out with the posse after the missing Catherine Holly.

'We found her clothes wedged in between these two rocks, blood all over them, like maybe somebody was trying to hide them. Can't bury nothing up here, so I guess it was the best they could do,' Tope explained. He looked apologetic when he said, 'There weren't no corpse, but I doubt she was taken along naked. All this blood probably paints none too pretty a picture of what happened. They probably had their fun and then killed her. Wolves got her, most likely, or other critters. They wouldn't leave much.'

Holly squinted up into the bright, harsh sky. It was noon. It had taken less than half a day to ride up there. 'You think after busting out of jail, killing the town marshal and his three deputies, taking the bank and then high-tailing it with a posse after them, you think these men stopped for some fun — this close to town?'

The sheriff shot Holly an anxious look, then cleared his throat before answering. 'Well now, don't get all riled because I mention it, but Mrs Holly was a damned attractive woman. Turn any man's head. And, anyways, they had time to do their business before we ever got started.'

Holly looked over at the Paiute tracker's closed, impassive face. He'd talked with the man not long after arriving in town. 'They had time? Well, I guess they did, since it was a full day before your posse started out after them.'

'Hey, look now,' Tope protested, 'I was way over at the other end of the county, and the marshal and all three of his deputies were dead. It took time getting some men together.' Tope looked down at the stained rock. 'This is where we lost them. Never could pick up their trail again. Tukwa there found her things and we rode on a ways, but my jurisdiction pretty much ends beyond that range of hills. I got back to Stillwater and telegraphed warnings to all the towns they were likely making for. That was the most I could do under the circumstances.'

Holly looked around the bare, rugged hills that swept away in all directions:

hard country to find a trail, but not impossible for a good tracker like Tukwa. The Paiute was from the Agai Panina Ticutta tribe. His people had mostly lived along the borderlands of three states, Nevada, California and Oregon, but their lands had been seized back in '67. There was now a military reservation there called Camp McGerry. Holly had got a handle on Tukwa's character during their talk, and he knew the man would have tracked the murderers for as long as it took. He had obviously been ordered back to town with the rest of the posse.

Holly might have asked why Tope hadn't used the Paiute's skills better, and why he'd given up so easily. Holly himself would have damned all that jurisdiction nonsense to hell, and continued the pursuit. But he didn't ask, because he knew the answer.

The look of the man told its story. The soft, dandified clothing and smooth-shaved baby cheeks and over-cultivated hair, it all marked him for a businessman and local politician; a man who used his position as county sheriff to further his ambitions and enlarge his personal wealth, and to hell with enforcing the law or protecting the folks that appointed him. He was never going to put much more effort into a manhunt than he had to.

Perhaps sensing Holly's thoughts, Tope said, 'I reckon they just had too much of a lead on us.'

'But they wouldn't have had that lead,' Holly snarled, 'if you'd managed to shift your elegantly trousered backside a mite quicker.'

A flush darkened the sheriff's face. 'Just who do you think you're addressing, sir? I know you're upset about your brother and his wife, but that's no excuse for such damned insulting behaviour.'

Holly's eyes narrowed. 'I'm upset, right enough. Upset that my kinfolk got murdered and some bone-idle, soft-skinned, money-raking excuse for a lawman couldn't get hisself bothered enough to do his job and bring the killers in. If I was to get any more upset you might be joining my brother's wife in providing nourishment for the critters.'

'You're threatening me?' Tope blustered. 'You actually have the gall to threaten a legally appointed county official? I heard about you, Holly, although not from your brother. I heard you were a brutal, uncompromising and thoroughly unpleasant sort of man, about one step away from being as lawless as the men you hunt. I guess I can understand James not ever wanting to talk much about you. I've a mind to arrest you right now.'

Holly's smile was slow and grim. 'Why don't you try that, Tope, and we'll see what happens next.'

Tukwa and Sefton backed the horses away; they'd signed on to help find Catherine Holly, not to mix up in anything like this. Holly's pose was relaxed and easy, but his eyes were chips of blue ice, his lips curled in a dangerous mirth. Tope faced him down for a few seconds, before remembering his usual habit of self-preservation at all costs.

'I guess I can let it pass this time,' he said. 'The loss of loved ones can make people act a little crazy.'

Holly nodded his approval. 'You're a wise man, Sheriff. You just made a decision to keep on living.' He retrieved his horse from Sefton. Once mounted he swung the pinto around towards Tope and said, 'We'll head back into town, and along the way you'll tell me all you know about the jailbreak and how it happened, leaving nothing out.'

Tope nodded to the other men to mount up. As he heaved himself up into his saddle he allowed a long breath to escape his lips. It took a while for his heart to slow its panicked drum-roll.

★   ★   ★

Holly sat in his brother's office, in his brother's chair behind his brother's desk, and his brooding eyes were fierce with both anger and regret. The town marshal's office was small and neat — James had always been neat. Drawers were closed, papers squared on the desk, the remaining rifles snug in their rack; even the wanted posters had been hung with sharp precision. There was just one thing missing.

Holly had searched the tiny bunk room at the back, and it wasn't the sort of item he'd expect to see left in any of the four cells. Where was it then? He would have figured James to have a picture of his wife somewhere in the office, but there was no sign of one. Maybe he hadn't gotten around to it, and any photographs had gone when the house burned down.

He was going to send me a picture, Holly thought. I guess he never got the chance, and anyways, he figured I'd show up one of these days, when I got around to it.

Lifting the creased and stained letter lying on the desk, Holly read it again.

My dear old Nate,

You haven't answered my letter so I hope it reached you all right, wherever you are. If it didn't, then I surely hope this one catches up to you. Me and Catherine is married a month now and we'd have been pleased if you'd made the wedding, but I guess you were out hunting law-breakers and such, and getting into trouble like you always do. Lisa couldn't make it neither, being busy with schooling all them children and bringing up her own brood as well. She wrote me that there's another baby due. A boy she hopes, since her and Connor has three girls already.

I wish you could see my Catherine. She's got the face of an angel, hair the colour of spun gold and eyes that sparkle like precious gems. I know you're going to laugh when you read such flowery romantic nonsense. I never was much good at describing things and I reckon Catherine's beauty is beyond my powers, so I guess you'll have to come see for yourself. She has a nature close to your own I reckon, determined and strong and does things her own way and no one else's. I'm the luckiest cuss alive, and I hope you'll be here soon to witness the truth of it. In the meantime, I'll send you a photograph soon as I get one took that I can bear to part with.

Your little brother,
James.

Holly put the letter down and sat back in the chair, a dark scowl on his face. He silently cursed himself for a fool. Mrs Norton had been right. Family were too important to ignore. You never realized how important until something like this happened, and then it was too late. When had he and James last seen each other? Two years was it — maybe three? And he hadn't laid eyes on his sister, Lisa, since she'd married that lawyer fellow about ten years back.

Ten years. Hell! Where did the time go to?

Holly sat back in the chair and gave some thought to all he'd heard since arriving in town. James had been alerted to the arrival in town of a wanted man. The dodger was still on the board facing him, and Holly studied the broad, black-stubbled face of Silas Broome. The eyes were set way too close together. Either the artist who did the sketch wasn't very good or Broome was one deformed and ugly-looking cuss.

Figuring Broome to be either in the saloon, or in the livery stables if he was planning on staying a while, James and his deputies set out to arrest him. When they spotted him outside the bank holding a string of five horses, it was clear there was a robbery under way. When the other four robbers came out they found themselves facing a ring of guns aimed directly at them, and their mounts put beyond reach.

The names the five men gave were probably false, but one was known from the wanted dodger, and another was known to Holly from the description given. Spanish Jack Speck was a big beefy man all running to fat, with black moustaches and a sombrero with an elaborate silver band that he was never seen without. There were two little bells on the hatband, taken as trophies from some gambler he'd killed, or so it was said. The fancy hat had a hole in it that Holly once put there. At the time he'd regretted it not being the man's head, and he now regretted it even more. It was something he intended to set right.

The other three gave their names as Shilto, Hinks and Weaver. Jack Weaver had been the leader of the gang, and Holly had a good description of the man from a lady called Sarah Fennell. Most of the towns-folk had barely seen the men before James had them locked away, but Sarah owned an eating-place near the jailhouse, and she was paid by the town to supply meals for any prisoners.

Questioned by Holly, she'd said,

'That Jack Weaver was as charming a rogue as I ever laid eyes on; a twinkle in his baby blues and a ready smile and a jest on his lips; skin as fair as any girl and hair to his shoulders, as yellow as the corn. Oh, he had a wicked way with the ladies, that one. I nearly got to swooning myself, and I ain't swooned over a man in near on twenty years. The others weren't of no account, just saddle trash. The one called Shilto was a long skinny drink of misery, with two fingers missing on his left hand.'

When asked about Catherine Holly, Sarah's expression had darkened with grief. 'That poor little lady, taken by those animals — it don't bear thinking about. She was so quiet and reserved, but a lady with hidden depths, I always thought. They were such a handsome couple, your brother and Catherine. Anything I can do to help you find those murdering dogs, you just tell me, Marshal. That dandified excuse for a man, Leonard Tope, he sat in town long enough so they'd get away. Afraid of getting into a shooting fight, I reckon, and getting his hair all mussed.'

The men had been three days in the cells, waiting for the circuit judge and a transfer to the state prison, when the jailbreak happened. The only explanation was that one of the men had somehow got hold of a gun. James Holly was shot down where he stood outside Weaver's cell door, and the deputy present had been forced to unlock the cells before he too was killed. The men had taken rifles from the rack and gunned down the remaining two deputies as they ran down the street to the jailhouse.

Witnesses saw one of the men drag Catherine Holly out and take her into the livery stables. She must have been with her husband in the jailhouse when the break happened. The stables were close to the house James and Catherine were living in, and some witnesses said they saw Catherine break away and run into the house. As she was dragged back out the house went up in flames. It was supposed that an oil lamp was used, but why the house had been fired was a mystery, perhaps down to pure meanness or to provide a distraction while the others robbed the bank a second time. This time they got away with the money, and with Catherine Holly.

At least one of the men had taken a bullet during the escape. Some of the town's citizens had armed themselves and began firing on the gang as they rode out. A blood trail out of town showed that someone had hit their target, but the trail stopped soon enough, probably when the wound was crudely bandaged. It wasn't thought to have been fatal, since no body was recovered, unless it also had been disposed of by Tope's hungry critters.

As Holly considered all these matters, the door opened and the Paiute tracker came in. He wasted no time on polite greetings. 'You're going after them. I will go with you.'

Holly took his time in answering. He studied the man in the doorway. The

Paiute wore a patterned shirt of some coarse material, dark cavalry pants tucked into soft deerskin boots, and a cavalry-issue coat that indicated service as a scout. The broad red slash of a headband pulled a fall of shiny black hair from his face. Another sash at his waist held a broad-bladed hunting knife and a tomahawk; the wicked-looking iron cutting edge was about four inches from toe to heel, with a spiked poll and a long straight haft of hickory wood. The rifle he carried was a Sharps single shot carbine.

'Don't you want to get back to your people?' Holly asked.

'No one waits for me.' The words were spoken without emotion or explanation, and Holly asked for none.

There were only two Winchesters left in the rifle rack. The outlaw gang had taken the others. Holly threw one to the Paiute. 'Tukwa, I'd be right pleased to have you along, but the Winchester will prove a better weapon than that carbine. Too much time has been wasted already. There are two Jacks in this deck that we know of; Weaver is one, and I got me an idea where we can find the other gentleman. Spanish Jack Speck has habits that are known to me. We leave at dawn.'

4

Spanish Jack Speck

Followed by catcalls from the bar, the black-haired woman on the staircase turned for a second to shake her ample bust in that general direction. There was a serious threat to the stitching on her low-cut blouse, but it seemed much appreciated by the gentlemen gathered there. The woman sashayed on up the stairs, only dropping her hip-swaying motion when she turned on to the first floor corridor, when her body slumped with tiredness. Two rows of facing doors, five apiece, were dimly lit by a single lamp halfway along. The last door on the left led into her room, and she'd barely entered when a hand closed around her throat.

'Not a sound, Elena, or your windpipe won't be no more use to you.'

She nodded, recognizing the gruff voice. Elena Parrada knew better than to mess with Nathan Holly. He eased her across the room close to where a table was set by the window, holding an oil lamp. He glanced outside, across an ornately carved wooden balcony and into the street. It was dark outside, and there were few people moving about, mostly entering and leaving the saloons and eating-places, but paying no attention to the first-floor room.

Finally removing his arm, he turned the lamp up just enough so Elena could see the mean look in his cold blue eyes. Elena had never liked Holly's eyes. There was no gentleness in them, and no appreciation for the physical attributes that made other men bend so easily to her will.

'What are you doing here, Marshal? What do you want?'

'You know what I want, so don't play games. Where is he?'

Back in Stillwater, Holly had a notion as to where Spanish Jack Speck might

49

be headed after the escape and bank robbery. It had been confirmed when Tukwa told him he'd done a little more tracking after Tope had abandoned the pursuit. The five men had separated, once clear of the posse, and one of them had swung a wide loop back towards the south. Holly figured Speck would be running for Mexico, but before he crossed over from Arizona he'd likely make a stop in the border town of Nogales. There was a saloon girl called Elena Parrada that Speck was particularly sweet on, and he wouldn't pass up the chance of enjoying her charms for a few days. Also, Speck had friends in that town and he'd feel safe there.

'I haven't seen him,' Elena answered, not bothering to ask who the marshal was talking about. She cast an anxious look towards the door and Holly caught it, despite the darkened room. The sound of jingling bells that followed a moment later had Holly's hand pressed hard over Elena's mouth.

Speck was inside the room a few seconds before his eyes adjusted to the gloom. He started to speak Elena's name, then he saw the marshal's huge frame standing behind her. His gun hand twitched, but it was no more than a reflex action; he knew he'd never make it. The Colt in Holly's right hand, the one not holding on to Elena, seemed twice the actual size with its dark eye pointing directly at his chest, ready and willing to wink him a bullet at the first wrong move.

Easing his hand away from the gun, Speck said, 'Holly, it is you. This is such a surprise. What do you want, *hombre?* That is a very unfriendly thing you do to Elena. I thought you had more respect for women.'

Holly released Elena and told her to go sit on the bed, before motioning Speck closer to the lamp. 'Turn it up,' he said. Speck did so. Standing in the full glow of the lamp he was uncomfortably exposed before Holly's merciless eyes. 'Unbuckle the gunbelt and drop it

51

to the floor, and do it carefully.'

Once the gunbelt hit the floor, Holly said, 'There were five of you. Where did the other four take off to?'

Speck feigned confusion while his eyes danced around the room, seeking some method either of escape or of distracting the marshal for a few vital seconds. 'Five of us? What are you talking about, *hombre?* Five of us? I rode in alone only a few days ago. Who are these other four you speak of?'

'A town called Stillwater,' Holly said. 'You killed the town marshal and his deputies, kidnapped and murdered the marshal's wife, and robbed the bank.'

Speck threw his arms wide, expressing amazement. 'You got the wrong *hombre*, Marshal. I never been in this — what you call this place? Stillwaters? — I never been there. As God is my judge, I never heard of the place.'

Holly allowed a silence to settle. Speck attempted a look of injured innocence, while his shifty eyes continued their frantic search of the room.

Once or twice they rested on Elena, and it was clear to Holly that he was trying to pass an unspoken message. If he was hoping Elena would risk herself to distract the marshal, he'd wait until hell froze over. Holly knew Elena Parrada well enough. She'd risk her neck for no one.

When Holly finally broke the silence it was in a low, chill voice. What he said told Speck that his life hung by a thread. 'The town marshal was James Holly. He was my brother.'

In all his three days in the jailhouse, Speck had never heard the town marshal referred to by his full name. He was visibly shaken and swallowed nervously as the full import of the revelation sank in. It changed whatever chances he'd thought he had. If he didn't bargain for his life, Holly would kill him. He might do it anyway.

'I didn't know. It wasn't me who shot him, I swear to you.'

'Where were the others going, after you all split up?'

'I don't know, I swear.' As Holly eased the hammer on the Colt to full cock, Speck cried out frantically, 'No, wait, don't shoot! I don't know where they all went, we were to lie low for a while, throw off anyone who might still be following. I was finished with them, but there was a job they were going to pull later on, somewhere up north. They were planning on meeting up again.'

'Another job? Why? You had the money from the bank in Stillwater.'

'They did the bank for travelling money, except it went wrong for them. They didn't know there was a dodger out on Broome, so I guess they're not so damned smart after all. I met up with them just before they hit town. I was along for the bank robbery, but that was all. This other thing I don't know about.'

'Then I guess you're no further use to me.'

Speck raised his palms in a defensive reflex. 'Hold on! Please, *hombre*! I got one more very important piece of information that you'll need if you want to find them, but you got to bargain for it.'

'What is it?'

'Not so fast. You got to swear you'll just take me in and leave me to the law here in Nogales, and not kill me. I know you, Holly, if you say you'll do it you'll keep your word, no matter how much you'd like to put a slug in me.'

Holly knew he was figuring he had friends in town, maybe even among the local peace officers. It was the reason Holly hadn't informed the marshal's office he was in town, looking for Speck. It was the best play Speck could make, and Holly would have to accept it if he wanted the information Speck had. He sighed deeply, about to agree to something that went so completely against the grain.

'All right, Speck. I promise I won't kill you and I'll hand you over to the law here in Nogales. You have my word, but what you got to tell me better be good.'

Speck nodded. Satisfied with the marshal's words, he said, 'They were to meet one month after we parted, up in northern Nevada, in a town called Logan on the Marys River. They invited me in on whatever they had planned, said they needed as many guns as possible. I said I would join them there, but I never would have. That's all I know, but it should be enough. You know where to find them, *hombre*, and I hope they kill you good.'

'One more question. Who gunned my brother down, and what was done with his wife?'

Speck opened his mouth to answer, but a sudden hammering at the door stopped him. A voice called out, 'Jack! You in there with Elena? I been sent to tell you, Nathan Holly was seen in town, not an hour ago. You better skin on out of here, my friend.' There was more hammering, and the door, not properly closed, swung wide.

The man who stood framed there was stocky and short. The moment his eyes fell on Holly he went for his gun. 'Don't do it!' Holly snapped, but the man had his sidearm drawn and was bringing it up fast, cocking the hammer ready to shoot.

Holly's Colt spat flame and thunder, the noise deafening in the enclosed space. Two slugs hammered the man back out of the room, his own shot bringing dust and wood chips down from the ceiling as he fell. Holly swung back on Speck just as he hurled the oil lamp. Holly stepped back and the lamp exploded against the floor between them, throwing up a sheet of blazing oil.

Elena screamed and jumped off the bed, pressing against the back wall. Holly snatched blankets from the bed and threw them over the blaze, stamping it down. It took only seconds, but it was all Speck needed to snatch up his gunbelt and step out of the window on to the balcony. He fired a random shot back through the window to discourage pursuit. It thudded into the wall above Elena's head, bringing fresh screams.

'Cut it out!' Holly snarled. 'You ain't hurt! Stomp on that blanket and make sure the fire's out.'

Wary of more shots coming his way, Holly ducked his head out of the window. Speck was down at the corner of the building, clambering over the rail and then dropping to the street. He stopped only long enough to get off two rounds in the marshal's direction, before taking to his heels. As Holly climbed out of the window, Speck stopped running and fired once more. Chunks of rail flew apart under the impact, causing Holly to flatten against the wall. Thick smoke was drifting through the window now, obscuring both men one from the other. By the time Holly had waved the smoke away and chanced another look Speck was out of sight. Holly stepped over the damaged rail and dropped to the ground.

Speck had been running south,

towards the livery stables most likely. Holly followed cautiously, both the single-action and Navy revolver drawn and cocked. Speck would be in a desperate hurry to quit town, and was heading into the stables to get his mount, but he might also figure an ambush to be the better play. The marshal paused at every alleyway between buildings, listening and peering down the length of them, trying to penetrate the darkness. A young couple out for a stroll saw the drawn firearms and scurried away.

He was close to the livery stables, darkened alley-ways on either side, when the ruckus broke out behind him. He didn't turn, figuring Elena hadn't managed to control the fire and the saloon was emptying in a panic.

There was a clatter to his left, boxes falling. He swung his guns in that direction, just as a large tomcat darted from the shadows. There were stores both sides of the alleyway. Someone had piled boxes in there, and the cat had been foraging. Behind him, the tinkle of tiny bells told him that the cat had been a fatal distraction. He knew he was a dead man even as he swung around. Speck had him dead to rights. But as he turned he saw the man stagger out of the shadows of the side street opposite, his eyes bulging and his gun hand empty. His pistol lay behind him.

Speck was making wild motions with his hands, trying to claw at his own back. He twisted around and Holly saw the tomahawk lodged between his shoulder blades. As he fell dying, the hat bells singing his demise, Tukwa emerged from behind him and pulled the tomahawk free, finishing Speck with a savage blow to the neck that almost severed his head.

The Paiute had been waiting in the stables for Holly, and had clearly seen Speck's intended ambush.

Holly nodded his thanks, but wished the Paiute hadn't been quite so hasty in killing Speck. He'd badly wanted to know who pulled the trigger on his brother, and how the prisoners had got their hands on a gun. If it was Speck who'd killed James he'd already paid the price, and if it wasn't — well, the answers were waiting in Logan.

He looked back along the street. The first floor of the saloon was ablaze and crowds of people were milling about, shouting and trying to organize some firefighting strategy.

'I think we'll leave the good citizens of the town to deal with things,' Holly said. 'Our presence might not be appreciated, not with two dead men and the saloon set alight.'

With Tukwa following he headed into the livery stables, anxious to be gone.

5

The Red Eyed Captain

The long ride back into Nevada and north towards the Marys River territory was grim and mostly silent. Holly had known Paiutes who were stoic and disinclined to run off at the mouth, but riding with Tukwa was like having a stone carving for company. He responded to comments and observations with either grunts or as few words as covered the subject. One remark about why he'd brought a bow along, when he had the Winchester, got a short answer.

'Sometimes silence is better.'

Holly wasn't too sure if that referred to himself and his attempts at conversation, or if it had a more serious and sinister meaning. Tukwa had certainly been silent when he'd crept up behind Spanish Jack Speck in that side street.

Holly looked at the bow strung across the Paiute's saddle, sinew-backed and made of strong mountain cedar. The arrows in the tanned buckskin quiver would have sharpened stone points.

'This is taking a mite longer than we thought,' Holly tried again that evening as they made camp. 'I surely do appreciate your help, Tukwa, especially back there in Nogales. I'd have been drilled good if not for you. But you been giving a lot of your time to this, and I just want you to know that you ain't obliged to. If you got your own things that need doing, or if you got anyone waiting, I got no claim on any more of your time. I'll just be thanking you for coming this far.'

Tukwa didn't answer for so long that Holly reckoned he wasn't going to. The Paiute threw more brush on the fire, and in the dancing light his flat, impassive face looked both remote and cruel, as though his thoughts turned inward to some hatred that had burrowed deep and festered. When he did speak, his words were bleak and emotionless.

'The thing that needs doing is lost to me. No one waits, not for many winters past.'

Holly thought about this while he turned their meal on a makeshift spit above the fire. Tukwa had caught and skinned a prairie rabbit towards sundown. Holly poured a little whiskey over the rabbit and it hissed and spat.

'Give it some flavour,' he explained, taking a sip of the whiskey and offering the bottle. Tukwa took a long slug at it, and then shuddered as he handed it back.

After the rabbit had been consumed, the Paiute startled Holly by suddenly offering his story. 'I was scouting for the army out of McGerry,' he said, 'chasing gun-runners and renegades. I did this while my people were starving. It was a bad winter and supplies were not getting through. I had been gone many moons, and did not know that my people were being cheated of what little they had. The government men were taking their food to sell to the whites in the towns. A small band of Paiute went on a raid, killed some settlers. While I was scouting along the border a cavalry patrol, close to the reservation, came across a band of Paiute. They had been forbidden weapons, but they needed to hunt if they were to live. They weren't the warriors the patrol was seeking, but they killed them anyway, all of them, women and children and old men. My woman and my sons were among them.'

Holly nodded his understanding. It was a story repeated too many times in too many places. Hatred between the white settlers and the Indians often burned red-hot and young army officers, fresh from the Eastern military academies, had little experience and little inclination to understand the desperation of a people forced from their own land and crowded on to reservations not fit for the purpose. When chasing down hostiles they saw all Indians as the enemy.

'What did you do, Tukwa?'

'There was a captain in charge of the patrol. I had met with him before, a strange-looking man with long white hair and bad eyes. You have hard eyes, Holly, but it is the strength of your will that I see in them, not a need to do evil. This man had one eye with blood in it, as red as fire, as red as war. The other was as black as the night. There was no mercy in those eyes. He had a scar beside the red eye. One time, someone had tried to close his eyes for ever.'

'What was he called, this man?'

'His name was Captain Joshua Creelock. I made a blood oath to kill this man. I looked for him, but he too had left the army after the massacre. I searched but could not find him. Now I live apart from my people, in shame at my failure to spill his blood in payment for the wrong he did.' Tukwa lifted his face to Holly, so that the marshal could see his eyes and read the truth of his words there. 'So I will ride with you,

Holly, and help you kill these men, so your loved ones are avenged and my soul is not so empty.'

Holly shook his head. 'It's not about revenge, Tukwa. These men are thieves and murderers. Even had it not been my family, I'd still be bringing them to justice. Killing strangers won't ease your pain, but I welcome your company if you still want to ride with me.'

'I will ride with you,' Tukwa said, and his dark eyes told the marshal that he wasn't entirely believed. He wasn't sure he believed it himself, and that caused him a measure of unease. He was a lawman, and personal feelings didn't enter into his duty. So he told himself, and he reckoned he'd have to live with that.

★   ★   ★

Logan was a bustling town, busy with every type of commerce Holly could imagine. The day he and Tukwa rode in an icy wind cut at them like a sharpened blade. Fat flakes of snow swirled around as though undecided about a heavier fall.

'First thing we got to do is get you some winter clothing,' Holly said, as they tended their mounts in livery stables on the far edge of town.

The owner was a wiry little man with a moustache too large and bushy for his small face. 'The name's Jenkins. That'll be two bits each for the night, mister, unless you're planning on staying longer?' He eyed Tukwa as he said this.

'It's hard to tell how long our business might take, Mr Jenkins,' Holly answered. 'You got a decent hotel in town where we might put up for a few days?'

Jenkins looked at Tukwa again and slowly shook his head. 'No offence, mister, but you won't be staying at no hotel with him. Paiute, ain't you? I got no feelings against your kind myself, but my lack of animosity ain't exactly widely shared, if you get my meaning.' At the flare of anger in Holly's eyes he added, 'I got a little room at the back of the stables, for use of occasional help when I need someone here all night. I got me a house a couple of streets over. If you like, your friend can bunk in there until your business is done.'

Holly looked at Tukwa, and the Paiute nodded his agreement.

'You can eat down at Molly Pedlow's place. She's a strong-minded Christian lady and has got no prejudice against Indians. She taught school to Paiute children for some years. The marshal's a good man too. You won't get no trouble from him if you keep your nose clean.'

'I'm acquainted with Sam Sugar,' Holly told him. 'I got to see him before we eat. Tukwa, you stay here, get the horses settled and I'll be back soon.'

As Holly unfastened his heavy sheepskin coat, Jenkins took in the US marshal's badge and the weapons. Besides the single-action Colt and the heavy weight of the Navy revolver, Jenkins looked at the Winchesters and the mountain cedar bow and gave a low whistle. 'Whatever your business is, I guess you can take care of it with all that artillery.'

Holly didn't answer. He headed on down the street to inform Sam Sugar that he was in town, and to warn that it might get messy if the men he was hunting made a fight of it.

Sugar greeted him solemnly, offered his sympathies for Holly's loss, and told him he'd help in any way he could. Holly was thankful that his old friend wasn't another Leonard Tope. Sugar might be ageing, but he was a professional.

'We're keeping an eye on all new arrivals in town. This feller Broome is the only one we got a good description of, there being a dodger out on him and all. If he rides in we'll know it.'

Holly thanked him. 'If Speck was telling the truth, they're supposed to be meeting here sometime in the next week or so. Tukwa and I will hang around, but we'll try not to be too visible. You got any notion of a job they could be planning hereabouts?'

Sugar grunted and chewed on his moustache for a moment. 'Could be the bank, I guess, but if it is they're making a mistake that'll cost them some blood. This town can deal with any outlaw gang that numbers less than a cavalry regiment.'

Holly grinned. 'I don't doubt it, Sam. Well, if you get any ideas let me know. Right about now I got a hankering to try this Molly Pedlow's cooking.'

With Sugar's assurances that he was in for a treat, Holly went back to the stables to collect Tukwa. The Paiute attracted a lot of attention, some of it curious and some of it hostile, as he followed the marshal, first into a general store where Holly outfitted him with a heavy sheepskin coat similar to his own, then directly across the street to a spacious eating-house that bore the simple legend 'Molly's Place' above the doors.

Six long trestle-tables were set out in

rows of two, with three curtained booths set to the rear. The vast interior was dark and gloomy unless you were just shy of the windows, but lit oil lamps hung suspended above each table. A nice touch, Holly thought, seeing as he liked to know what he was eating. Flowered wallpaper adorned the walls, which were hung at intervals with Bible passages and illustrations from various stories, mostly Old Testament. The commandments took pride of place above an elegantly carved reception desk, with the kitchen just beyond.

The place was crowded, barely a seat not filled. Holly reckoned that both Jenkins and Sam were right about the quality of Molly Pedlow's cooking and her nature, as she greeted both the marshal and Tukwa with equal courtesy. She was a large woman, with thickly curling iron-grey hair pulled back in a bun, plump red cheeks and a wide smile filled with strong white teeth. She led them to two spaces at the second table along the far wall, close to one of the curtained nooks. As Tukwa took his seat next to the marshal, the man on the other side of him stood up abruptly, shot a look of disgust at the Paiute and walked out, his meal unfinished.

'Your loss, mister,' Molly shouted after him. 'And I don't just mean the food.'

She took Holly's order and scurried out back. Two other ladies were serving and Holly heard the clatter of plates and cutlery from the kitchen, and Molly's voice giving instructions. A wonderful, mouth-watering aroma arrived just before the food, and the second it was placed before them Holly and Tukwa set in on the beef and dumplings.

They were just finishing, and Holly's thoughts were turning to the apple pie adorning other plates, when the curtain over the nearest booth was pulled back for an instant. A thin face glanced out at the room, narrowed eyes searching. It was the hand that held the curtain that caught Holly's attention. He stiffened as he took in the missing two fingers beside the thumb. The curtain dropped back into place.

Holly eased up from the table, whispering to Tukwa, 'You see that curtained booth? Follow me all casual like but be ready for a fight.' He handed the Navy revolver to the Paiute.

As they made their way past the other diners Holly's eye caught the framed commandments next to the kitchen door.

'Thou shalt not kill!'

I'll surely do my best, Holly promised.

6

Vengeance is Mine

There were two men seated in the booth. They were startled speechless as the curtain was roughly pulled aside and armed men pushed their way in. The skinny one seemed frozen for a moment, before dropping his good hand under the table.

'Don't do it!' Holly warned. 'Unless you want to lose more than fingers.' When the hand reappeared, he said, 'I guess you're the one calling himself Shilto. That's the name you were going under back in Stillwater.'

The thin face twisted in both innocence and confusion. Once over the shock he found his voice again. 'Shilto? I think you got the wrong man, mister. My name is Long, Henry Long. I never heard of no Shilto, and I never been to no place called Stillwater. Now, I'd be right pleased if you'd get that gun out of my face.'

The performance was less than convincing. Shilto's eyes were darting all over the place, but resting for seconds at a time on his companion. The other man looked like a sodbuster, burly, with big beefy hands and short brown curly hair. His face would have been pleasant but for the ugly twist to the mouth. From descriptions given, Holly recognized the man as Hinks. Both men were searching for an edge, passing unspoken words, but the guns occupying the small booth with them gave only two options; surrender or sudden death. Shilto seemed crazy enough to try — Holly had faced the type before — but Hinks didn't look like he'd chance a bullet. The man was badly shaken; fear had drained the blood from his face and he was staring at the Paiute in something close to panic.

'There were four of you meeting here

in Logan,' Holly said. 'The other two are Broome and Weaver. Are they in town, or are you two waiting for them to show up?'

Shilto raised the maimed hand. 'Mister, I swear to you, I don't know what you're talking about. I just came in for a good hot meal along with my friend here.' Looking over Holly's shoulder, he raised his voice, 'Hey there, ma'am, could you please go get the marshal in here. These fellows are threatening my friend and me, and we never saw neither one of them before.' He stared at Tukwa. 'You allow savages in here, pointing weapons at innocent folk?'

Molly Pedlow came bustling over, her good-natured smile wiped clean by what she saw. 'Gentlemen, I don't allow this sort of thing in my establishment. You put those guns away right now.'

'I'm afraid we can't do that,' Holly said. He pulled his coat back to show his badge. 'I'm a US marshal and these are wanted men. I'm taking them in, but first I need some information from them.'

'You ain't the law around here,' Molly snapped. 'I already sent one of my girls to fetch Marshal Sugar. He'll be here very shortly, but in the meantime I must ask you all to leave.'

'All right, Miss Pedlow, we'll be leaving with our prisoners. With our guns out and with these men disarmed.' Holly took a step back from the booth. 'Both of you ease on out and drop your gunbelts.'

Hinks and Shilto exchanged glances before starting out of the booth. Hinks was cowed, but Shilto watched Holly and Tukwa carefully as he unbuckled and dropped his gunbelt, hoping for the chance of a move against them. But the armed men never relaxed their vigilance for a moment, and he scowled at Hinks as they gathered up the guns, as though it was his partner's fault they were in this fix.

'Before we go, I'll repeat my question,' Holly said. He aimed his Colt at

Hinks, pulling it to full cock as he said, 'Where are Broome and Weaver? Are they here in Logan?' He couldn't take a chance on the other two skinning out of town once they knew their friends were in the jailhouse.

Tukwa moved towards Hinks, his cruel eyes unnerving the man. 'You answer,' he said, drawing the broad-bladed hunting knife. Hinks stared at it coming towards him like he was watching an uncoiling rattlesnake. Lamp light danced along the blade.

Molly Pedlow shouted, 'Here, you stop that right now. Not in my place.'

But Hinks started to talk, the words spilling out in panic. 'Weaver's gone on up to Lazarus. Broome ain't here yet. We was just waiting around for him to show.'

Shilto shouted, 'Shut up, Hinks, you no-good streak of yellow pus! You don't tell them nothing!'

'He already has,' Holly said. 'All right, let's leave this good lady in peace. Outside, the both of you.'

He and Tukwa escorted the two men past a scowling Molly Pedlow, the Paiute carrying the dropped gunbelts over one shoulder. They were watched by only a dozen or so diners. Most had left the premises once guns were pulled. Holly regretted any damage done to Molly's business; she seemed a nice enough lady, but he'd had no choice.

They were almost at the door when a man entered, saw Shilto and Hinks, and declared loudly, 'I been all over town looking for you two. Just got in and I thought you'd left without me.'

Holly instantly recognized Broome, just as Broome saw that his friends were unarmed and that the man behind them had his gun drawn. He pulled his pistol as Holly stepped clear of the prisoners.

Twin explosions deafened those closest to the sudden gunfight. Holly had fired a fraction before Broome, hammering a slug into Broome's chest. Broome's shot went wide as he staggered under the impact, the bullet hitting Hinks. It entered through his right eye and blew the back of his head open. Dark blood sprayed across the reception desk and the flowered wallpaper behind it. He went down like an emptied sack.

Broome was badly hit, but he didn't go down. He swayed backwards, firing again. Chairs crashed over as the remaining patrons tried to get away from the fight. There were yells and screams and someone banging across a table in boot heels, desperate to get clear. One of Broome's bullets shattered an oil lamp, another smashed plates on one of the tables.

A plump, red-cheeked man in a rumpled suit slammed into Tukwa, almost knocking him over. For a moment he was between the Paiute and his prisoner, and it was all Shilto needed. He was on top of Tukwa and wrestling him to the floor the second the fat man was clear. The gunbelts clattered to the floor close beside them.

Holly put Broome down with two more slugs, before swinging back to the

81

struggle behind him. Tukwa was beneath Shilto's skinny frame and Shilto had clawed a pistol out of the gunbelts. Shilto had a wiry strength, but didn't stand a chance of overcoming the muscular Tukwa. The gun made all the difference. He was pushing against the Paiute's restraining arm, inching the barrel closer to Tukwa's head.

Holly stepped over and pressed the barrel of his Colt against Shilto's temple. He was about to order the man to drop the pistol, when he did just that. The gun fell from suddenly lifeless fingers and the man slumped against the Paiute.

'Hell no!' Holly moaned. 'You killed him!'

Tukwa rolled the dead man off him, the knife still deeply imbedded in his heart. There was no apology on the cruel face, impassive even though he'd been seconds from death. Holly couldn't blame him. Shilto might have fired anyway, even with the marshal's gun to his temple. He'd been mean enough to do it. But Holly had wanted to question at least one of these men, and now all three were dead.

As Tukwa got to his feet, Holly became aware of the frantic commotion all around him. People were milling about, shocked into agitated, confused and aimless motion by the sudden eruption of violence. Heavy curtains had been thrown over the shattered oil lamp. Crowds were gathering at the door, but only a few ventured inside. He looked over at the elegant reception desk and Molly Pedlow, her face streaked with blood. For a second he thought she'd been hit, but then he realized it was from Hinks. Her face under the red mask was white with shock. Behind her the wallpaper dripped red.

As Sam Sugar pushed into the room with his deputies, Holly's eyes rested on a Bible passage. 'Vengeance is mine, sayeth the Lord.'

This day, vengeance was mine, Holly thought, but it wasn't what I wanted.

A voice way back in his head asked him if he was entirely sure of that.

'So the trail has gone cold?' Sugar asked.

They were gathered in the marshal's office the following morning; Sugar, Holly and two deputies. The Paiute was saddling the horses, preparing to leave.

'We got one piece of information,' Holly replied. 'Hinks said that Weaver had gone on up to Lazarus.'

'Lazarus — that's that new silver town, used to be called the 'Crazy Mike'. This new feller, Lester Ryle, he got some surveyors in, found richer seams than old Mike Barton ever did, got some real fancy equipment up there to mine it. That town he started is growing fast. I have business up there myself in a day or two, depending on a certain delivery being made.'

Holly nodded. 'You remember the Norton family. You met them a while back, after that incident in the hills. They were starting up a general store in Lazarus.'

'I know the Nortons. So you reckon on finding the last of these murderers in Lazarus?'

'If he's still there, I'll find him.'

A hammering started up somewhere down the street.

'Undertaker,' Sugar said. 'Fixing coffins to bury those fellers you and the Paiute sent to their happy hunting grounds.'

'I'm sorry for the trouble we caused you. Molly Pedlow seems on the warpath herself this morning. I seen her from the hotel, storming in here.'

Sugar shrugged. 'Molly's a good sort. She'll get over it. I'll get some grief from the citizen's committee, but nobody got dead that didn't have it coming.' His mouth twitched above the stained white moustache, and there was an amused twinkle in his eye. 'Still, you gave us about a year's worth of excitement last evening, so I guess it'll do us a while. Things is always more peaceable when you're not around, Nate.'

Holly got to his feet. 'You're a good man, Sugar, but I guess we caused you enough trouble. We'll be riding out within the hour.'

He offered his hand and Sugar took it, turning more serious. 'I wish you luck with this last feller. You be right careful, Nate. He sounds like a slippery one, and they're the worst. You can't always see them coming.'

Sam Sugar's words would prove more prophetic than he knew.

7

The Regulators

The body was partly eaten, the face almost entirely removed. It had been left in a grave too shallow to prevent the wolves from getting at it. There was no marker of any kind.

'He was shot to death,' Holly said, examining the corpse.

He raised his face to the wind coming down from the north, carrying the promise of snow on its frozen breath. The body had to be prised from the earth by both men. A rime of frost lay across the ruined face.

'Maybe he was robbed,' Tukwa said.

Holly had come down to the river for water after a restless and cold night's sleep. They'd got a good blaze going with some pine kindling the previous evening, but hadn't thought a shelter necessary. A good supply of firewood had been gathered, mostly dead wood caught up in the branches of trees so it would be dry enough, but it hadn't been enough. Towards dawn the fire had burned too low to keep out an increasingly bitter chill. Holly hadn't been inclined to go looking for more wood and had dozed off again. When he'd finally awakened, with aching bones and bloodshot eyes, Tukwa had already got the fire relit. Holly went to fetch water to get some strong coffee going, and it was then that he'd discovered the body, buried close to the river and just inside the tree line.

'He crossed someone up real bad, that's for sure. Could be someone wanted to rob him, or it could be something else. We'll see if anyone's missing up at Lazarus. Better get what's left wrapped for travel. We'll hit town by noon I reckon.'

They ate a hurried breakfast of bacon and beans and broke camp. After splashing water over the embers of the fire and stirring them with a stick, Holly gathered the ashes in a cook pot and scattered them to the wind. He stood for a few moments, watching the dark clouds that rolled down across the forested ridges to the north of him like a shroud.

'The weather is going to get bad up there,' he said.

He felt something in his bones that was more than an ache brought on by the cold. He had always been able to sense trouble, a gift that had probably kept him alive for so long in his dangerous profession. He sensed it now, on the icy wind blowing down from Lazarus, and it concerned more than the fugitive he was hunting. He looked across the campfire to where the corpse lay, tightly wrapped in a horse blanket, and he felt a chill whisper of unease.

★ ★ ★

The town lay snug inside a crescent-shaped depression, junipers and pines still standing amongst the sprawling buildings. Except for the long, relatively straight main street, the rest seemed haphazardly sited, running off in all directions: wood frame buildings built around stone chimneys mostly. Behind the town Holly could just make out the stick and mud cabins of the miners; several hundred of them from what he could see through a misty haze enveloping the depression.

He and the Paiute sat their horses on a ridge above the town. Light flurries of snow blew around them, and the sky was the colour of bleached bones. The pinto shifted nervously, as though sensing something on the smoke-laden breeze. Lonely spirals of wood smoke were drifting into the sky, like souls lost in all the bleak emptiness that surrounded the little town. No one could be seen on the streets, no movement at all.

'Lazarus indeed,' Holly snorted. 'It'd take a miracle to bring any life to this place.' He turned to Tukwa and said, 'But I could be wrong. I guess we better ride on in, see if they got any law here we need to hitch up with.'

At the top of the main street there was a sign posted, telling any travellers that they were entering the town of Lazarus and were required to report to the local law. Fair enough, Holly figured, caution in this remote place being a sensible attitude.

There hadn't been anyone around while they rode down into the depression, but as they passed a skeletal, half-built wooden construction with a lantern burning over a doorless opening, a man stepped out of the shadows up ahead of them. He waited patiently for them to reach him, a Winchester lying idle across his folded arms. It was only when they reined in that he swung the rifle up towards them.

'Who are you folks?' the man barked. 'What you doin' up here?'

'Well, that don't sound too friendly a greeting,' Holly answered. 'I got a question of my own, which is who the hell are you, mister?'

'I'm the law, is who I am, and you better tell me right now what you want here, and why that Indian is riding with you.' He took a bead on Holly's head, his finger closing on the trigger. He had a narrow face, with a long jaw and squinting eyes.

Holly studied the man for a moment, finally deciding that he wasn't bluffing. What the hell was wrong with this town? The building he'd stepped out of had no sign saying it was the marshal's office, but it clearly was, if this man was to be believed. 'I'm the law as well, so I guess that makes us related. United States Marshal Nathan Holly, and what I'm doing here we can discuss inside, with a cup of hot coffee to thaw out me and my posse.'

The man scowled at Tukwa. 'That there is your posse?'

'Only one I need. Are you intending to invite us inside or not?'

'Bring them on in, Emmett.' The voice came from inside the building. It was deep and rasping, as though it had to force its way past some blockage. 'Let's get a look at them.'

Emmett stepped back up on the boardwalk and motioned them inside. Holly and Tukwa dismounted, tied their mounts to the hitching rail, and headed on in. There was a small entrance hall, with stairs to the left and the doorway to an office on the right. Emmett went and stood in the doorway, allowing Holly to pass but pushing his rifle into Tukwa's chest. 'Not you,' he snarled. 'We keep the dogs penned up in back.'

Tukwa tensed, and Holly said, 'What's that on your lip, mister?'

Emmett said, 'Huh? What's on my lip?' and reached up to his mouth, the rifle swinging down to his side.

Holly hit him hard and said, 'That is.'

As the man collapsed against the door, Tukwa stepped over him, his gun out and ready for more trouble.

'Easy, Tukwa,' Holly told him. 'I don't reckon we need to shoot up no lawmen, if that's what they are.'

A log fire was burning badly, hazing

the room with evil-smelling smoke, but Holly made out a spacious office with two desks, and where he would have expected to see a rifle rack there was a bookcase, filled to overflowing with well-thumbed volumes. There looked to be more rooms in the back, where the absent armoury might be located. A cavalry sabre resting on two pegs was the only visible weapon besides the men's sidearms. Two men sat at ease in chairs pulled close to the fire, despite the fug, with a third seated behind one of the desks, his feet up on top of it. All three wore dark suits and waistcoats. Of the man with his feet up, the smoke-haze hid his features, but the other two, despite their relaxed postures, had watchful, mistrustful eyes that held no welcome for the two strangers.

'I apologize for Emmett,' the man behind the desk said. 'He gets a mite over-zealous at times, and his lack of fine character traits includes a prejudice against your kind — Tukwa, wasn't that the name? And you, Mister United

States Marshal, maybe we could have your name as well.'

'Holly. Nathan Holly.'

'I knew you looked familiar. I remember you from Fort Smith, on the Arkansas border. I saw you bringing in prisoners a few times. So what are you doing up here, Marshal?'

'I don't recollect ever meeting you,' Holly said, trying to get a better look at the man. 'What was your business at Fort Smith?'

'We didn't actually meet. I was an army man back then.' He leaned forward out of the haze and Holly felt Tukwa's sudden tension at the long white hair and the scar beside the blood-filled left eye. 'Captain Joshua Creelock at your service, Marshal; now, what can I do for you?'

'We're up here looking for a fugitive and murderer. But first, may I ask what authority you and your men have here?'

'We're regulators, appointed to keep the peace here by the town's special constable, Mr Warren McQueen. He's

95

also the Lazarus Mining Company's lawyer and accountant.'

Holly looked out of the window at the silent, empty street. 'Keeping the peace here seems like it'd be an easy job for an eighty-year-old with shaky limbs and bad eyesight. It really needs four men, one a former officer in the army?'

Creelock returned his humour with a thin smile. 'It's quiet now with the men up at the mine, but it can get pretty wild when they all come storming in. This was a wide-open boom town before we were appointed, with a lot of drunken riots and frequent killings. And there are six of us, not four; enough to deal with any kind of trouble.' He waved towards the two seated men. 'That there's Walt Raine and Isaiah Hobb. Lamar LaVey and Zach Ponder are up at the mine, seeing there's no trouble. That gentleman on the floor is Emmett Marley, but I wouldn't be counting on a close friendship any time soon.'

Holly looked at the unconscious man. 'I'm sure he'll come around.'

Creelock nodded and his gaze shifted to Tukwa, the bloodied eye seeming to settle on him with malevolent intent. 'Your 'posse' seems a mite unsettled, Marshal. I see something in his eyes that I can't quite figure, but I find it oddly disturbing. Have we ever crossed trails before?'

For a moment Tukwa didn't answer, and Holly tensed himself for action. But then the Paiute said, 'I have never seen you before.'

Creelock kept his gaze on him for another second, before shrugging and saying, 'All right then.' He turned his attention back to Holly. 'So who is this man you're looking for, and why do you think he's here? It seems an odd place to run to.'

'He and four other men staged a jailbreak in Stillwater, murdered a town marshal and his deputies, abducted and murdered the marshal's wife and robbed the town's bank.'

'My goodness, they certainly were busy little bad men.' The thin lips twitched in amusement. 'They did all that in one day, in the one town? Where are the four you're not hunting, or are you saving them for later?'

The sick humour was calculated to get a reaction from him, Holly realized. Creelock was trying to get his measure. He said, 'They're all dead.'

Creelock sobered instantly. 'You killed them?'

'I killed them. Before he died, one of them told me the last of the gang was headed here. He was travelling under the name of Jack Weaver when he was jailed back in Stillwater, but he won't be using it now. He's a handsome devil, by all accounts, and charming with the ladies, hair to his shoulders, like your own but more yellow, and blue eyes and very fair skin. Has any stranger fitting that description been seen in town?'

'We get few strangers here, being out of the way and all.' He looked questioningly at his regulators. 'There's

98

no one that I can think of, but we'll keep an eye out, won't we, men? I'll ask Lamar and Ponder when they come back in.'

'Do you have cells in here?' Holly asked.

'Upstairs. This was built to be a store. Mr Ryle, the man who owns the mine and the town, he didn't reckon on needing no jailhouse, nor no full-time lawmen for that matter. When he realized his mistake he gave this place over to us. We added barred doors to two of the rooms upstairs, barred the windows and turned them into jail cells. There's only old Potter up there now. Every town has a drunk I guess, and he's ours; spends more time in a cell than out.'

'If we get our man we'll need the use of one of those cells.'

'You'll have to clear that with Mr McQueen.'

'No I won't. I'm a federal officer in pursuit of a wanted fugitive. As the local law here you're legally obliged to render all necessary aid when it's asked for.'

Creelock spread his hands in surrender. 'Very well, Marshal. I'm not too conversant with such niceties, only enforcement. I look to Mr McQueen for advice in such matters. In the meantime, if you're looking for someplace to stay, I recommend rooms over in the Silver Palace.'

'Thank you, we'll get our mounts stabled and head on over there.' Holly gestured towards the bookshelves. 'Someone sure likes his reading.'

'That would be me,' Creelock answered. 'I'm particularly partial to Mr Charles Dickens. I'm reading *The Old Curiosity Shop*. Are you acquainted with his works?'

'I've read some,' Holly said. 'But before you get too comfortable with Little Nell, we got a body outside needs taking care of. We found him shot to death, half-eaten by wolves and then froze solid. Somebody hadn't buried him deep enough, I guess. Are you missing any citizens, Captain Creelock?'

The reaction from Creelock and his regulators wasn't the storm of frantic activity that one would expect. Before any of them moved from their chairs they all exchanged looks that told Holly the frozen body wasn't a surprise to them, just its discovery.

Holly hadn't told them about Spanish Jack Speck and his information about a job that Weaver and his men were planning, obviously in Lazarus itself. He didn't know what was going on in this town, and he didn't know whom he could trust, if anyone.

One man he didn't trust was Captain Joshua Creelock.

As they left the body in the care of Creelock's men, and headed to the stables, Holly said, 'It would be a mistake to move too soon.'

'I will wait for your word, Holly,' Tukwa said. 'When it is time I will kill him.' He stopped walking and Holly saw the implacable hatred glittering in his dark eyes. 'And when that time arrives no one will stop the death I have saved for him. It has waited too many moons for his blood.'

Holly studied the Paiute for a moment, before nodding his acceptance. 'All right, Tukwa, I hear your words and I won't stand against you. The man I'm looking for is Jack Weaver. Captain Joshua Creelock is all yours, but I reckon you'll need some help with his regulators.'

8

The Silver Palace

Sited next to an impressive, but only partly built, stone monolith, the Silver Palace was the next largest structure in town, with wide double doors sited on both corners facing on to the main street. A deeper than usual boardwalk was shadowed behind elaborate colonnades carved with dancing cherubs, and the doors themselves were painted with generously endowed ladies kicking their heels up. Holly thought he recognized the style — there would be fancy wallpaper with dancing cherubs blowing trumpets, and a huge mirror over the bar with a massive gilded frame. The voice he heard as he pushed the doors open confirmed his suspicion.

'Where is that boy? He's never around when I need him. Here,

Danielle, you give those tables a real good wipe. The boys we get in here ain't all that particular, but I like a clean establishment. That corner looks like someone stabled their horse in there. Lucy, the mirror over the bar needs doing; it's so misted I can't hardly see my own face in it.'

The woman who bustled about the vast, airy room didn't see Holly and Tukwa enter. As she came to a stand-still, surveying her kingdom with a critical eye, Holly smiled his appreciation of her. Her softly generous figure was such that she could well have posed for one of the ladies painted on the doors. Her upswept hair was a fiery red, and her eyes of pure cat-green were said by some to glow in the dark. Below a pert nose, the full lips were slightly parted, with her tongue touching her upper teeth as though tasting some dainty morsel.

'Hello Shona,' Holly said. 'I see you ain't lost none of your charm since I seen you last.'

Shona Gordillo, daughter of a Spanish horse breeder and an immigrant Irish mother, was an old friend. As with Sam Sugar, their paths had crossed many times over the years. Her saloons and business enterprises popped up in boom towns and growing communities across several states.

She swung around at the sound of Holly's voice, a huge smile lighting her entire face. Shona was in her mid-forties at least, but seemed immune from any visible ageing; a possible side effect of the energy that crackled off of her like lightning got loose from its bottle.

'Nathan Holly, you old law-dog, I never can get shook of you.'

'And you never will. Are you hitched yet, or are you still waiting for that millionaire to come a-calling?'

'I'm still waiting for you, Nathan, once you get me that million.'

Holly chuckled. 'Unlikely on a marshal's pay, but if I do find me a fortune lying about somewhere I'll be calling your bluff. Then you'll have to change the decoration some — all them cherubs make my eyes hurt.'

Shona threw her arms around him and Holly pulled her in tight. 'Hey, let me breathe, you big buffalo,' she gasped. Pulling free she took him by the hand. 'Come on in back, I got a little nook for visitors.'

'You always did have a little nook, as I recall.'

'None of that bad talk in here, law-dog,' she admonished. 'I've grown all respectable since you saw me last.' Her gaze fell on Tukwa, still standing by the door. 'Is he lost or is he with you?'

Holly waved him over. 'He's with me. He's been helping me find some people. Tukwa, this is Shona Florida Dolores Gordillo, to give her the full title.'

'I'm right pleased to make your acquaintance, Tukwa. I assume that the people you're helping him look for would object to actually being found.'

The playfulness left Holly's face and

his tone was grim as he said, 'We already found four of them.'

Shona raised an eyebrow. 'Any left alive? No, of course there aren't. It was a foolish question.'

'The fifth one's still kicking. He's the one we're here to find. You remember my brother, James; you met him once over in Lovelock?'

'That's right. I had a nice little saloon there; sold it to some Eastern gent as I recall, for quite a bit of money. How is James? He was a right personable young man, as I recall. I even considered throwing you over for your brother.'

'He's dead, Shona. We're hunting the last of the men who killed him.'

Shona's expression became as grim as Holly's. 'You both come on in back. Tell me any way I can be of help.'

'We need rooms here for a start.'

'Hell Nathan, that goes without saying. My two best rooms are as unoccupied as the other ten. I was thinking that gambling man might put up here a few nights, once he sees how easy it is to take money from the miners; although they ain't been paid in a while, so pickings won't be so good until the money gets here.'

She pointed the man out. He sat way back in a corner, playing by himself with a deck of cards. He wore a shabby suit and a fancy red vest that had seen better days. The corner table was away from the windows and Holly couldn't make out his features, save for a thatch of fair hair that instantly caught his interest. Seeing he'd suddenly become of interest the man dropped his head.

'Do you know him, Shona?'

'I've seen him around in other towns and other saloons. He's a gambler, fetched up here this morning. His name's Nevins, I think.'

'He don't look too prosperous.'

'Maybe he don't play at cards too well.'

'Maybe he don't.' The fact that Shona knew the man didn't mean he hadn't been passing through Stillwater with his gang. As he followed Shona into the back parlour, Holly glanced back at the gambler. The man seemed uncomfortable with the notice being paid him. Holly reckoned he already had suspect number one.

Turning his gaze from the gambler, he shot an admiring glance towards the slender, dark haired Danielle as she cleaned the tables. 'I see you brought a couple of the girls with you,' he observed, taking in the blonde, bright-eyed Lucy as well.

Taking his arm, Shona turned him away. 'You leave those innocents alone. I'm woman enough for you, law-dog.'

'Ain't that the truth,' Holly admitted.

* * *

Holly's awakening was a deal more comfortable than it had been the previous morning. He stretched his length on the king-size bed and reached for Shona, but she was already gone.

'Saloon work starts a mite too early for me,' he muttered, heaving out from under the bedclothes into freezing air.

He washed and dressed quickly, thinking that if ever he was to settle down with a woman, he couldn't choose better than Shona Gordillo. Looking at his big, unhandsome face in the shaving mirror he grimaced, figuring that he'd be getting the best of the bargain. Shona had money stashed in Eastern banks, more than she ever let on, and what did a marshal have to offer? Meagre pay and an early grave, most likely. Anyway, he and Shona were too alike; both had a liking for the freedom to do whatever the hell they were inclined to, without having to answer to anyone besides themselves. If there were any decency-loving females in Lazarus to outrage, Shona had most likely succeeded by inviting Holly to share her rooms and her bed, and it wouldn't bother her the least little bit.

Stomping downstairs into the main salon, he saw Shona giving careful instructions to a young man with wide blue eyes and a shock of straw-coloured hair that fell uncombed over an unlined brow.

As Holly went over to them he heard Shona saying, 'Now try to remember, Billy, you have to trim all the lamps down here and up in the hallways, all right? And be mindful of what you're doing, no daydreaming.'

He seemed little more than a boy, with clear, unblemished skin and untroubled eyes that seemed unusually vacant as he listened to Shona with rapt attention. Glancing round for a second at Holly's approach, his placid attentiveness vanished, to be replaced by a startled nervousness. Ducking his head, he hurried off to his set tasks.

'Who is he?' Holly asked.

'Billy Dill? He does all the odd jobs around the saloon for me. You have to give him very careful instruction though, as his mind tends to wander a mite far off what he's supposed to be doing.'

'Where did you find him, and how long has he been here?'

The tone of Holly's question snapped

Shona's head round. 'He ain't your man, law-dog. He's way too young for a start.'

'He acts young, but he's old enough.'

Shona sighed. 'Holly, everyone knows that boy is somewhat simple-minded. I've been taking care he don't get into trouble as much as I've been paying him to work for me.'

'The sight of me sure got him all jumpy.'

'The sight of you would make a marble statue all jumpy. He's nervous of strangers is all.'

'You knew him before Lazarus?'

'Well, no — '

'So when did he fetch up here?'

Shona hesitated before giving a resigned shrug. 'About three weeks ago. He wandered in with the supply wagons from Logan. But he's all right, Nathan, so you just leave that boy alone. He's under my protection.'

Holly had to smile. 'Then I guess he's out of reach of all harm. You can be a fierce lady, Shona. There's some that have the scars to prove it. If I leave him alone can I expect some breakfast as a reward?'

Settling at the table in the back parlour he asked if Tukwa was about.

'He was down here the moment he heard me and the girls moving about. He ate as soon as we had food ready and then he lit out, but I don't know where.'

Holly was instantly concerned. Despite their understanding of the previous evening, he understood the rage that burned deep inside the Paiute, and the need to avenge his murdered family. Holly felt the same things himself, and had to constantly fight down the blaze so that it didn't consume his duties as a lawman.

Forcing his mind off Tukwa, he asked, 'Do you know if there's anyone missing here in town, or up at the mine?'

Shona paused in pouring his coffee. 'Not that I heard tell of. Why do you ask?'

'Tukwa and I found a body half buried in the snow, half eaten by wolves and all frozen solid. We brought him in and left him with Creelock and his regulators. They didn't seem surprised by our find.'

Shona almost spat. 'Captain Joshua Creelock — now there's trash for you. He ain't no lawman and he's brought nothing but trouble and misery to this town since him and them bully boys of his were appointed. I don't know what Lester Ryle was thinking.'

'Creelock said there was a problem with public order that he was hired to stop; shootings and such.'

'Yes, there was some trouble, but who was responsible is open to question. It wasn't from the miners or the towns-folk. Mostly it was strangers coming into town, and that was strange enough, since we're pretty much hid up here in the mountains. Creelock cleared them out, sure enough, and then he set about establishing a rule of iron that has every-one scared of him and his men.'

'Why doesn't this Lester Ryle get shot of him?'

'That you'd have to ask of Lester himself; he ain't been down from the mine in a week, so I haven't been able to put it to him myself.'

Holly started to say, 'Maybe I'll take a ride up to — '

Clear and sharp on the chill morning air, the sudden explosion of multiple gunshots stopped him in mid-sentence and got him moving fast for the door.

Outside, a gun battle was raging.

9

Two Suspects

Three of the regulators were strung along the main street, blasting away in the direction of the stables. Creelock was hanging back, deep in the shadows of the boardwalk outside his office door. Faces were pressed up against windows the length of the street. Only the regulators were doing any shooting, as no return fire was coming from the stables.

'What the hell is going on?' Holly demanded, striding out in the middle of the street.

'Better get off the street, Marshal,' Creelock advised. 'We got a horse-thief penned in there and we're trying to winkle him out. It's that Paiute you brought into town with you.'

'Who says he's a horse thief?'

'We got a witness he was trying to make off with several mounts from them stables.'

'Where is your witness?'

Creelock smiled, knowing Holly wouldn't believe him and not caring if he did or didn't. 'A man by the name of Henry Potter; he's very well respected around these parts and I'm bound to take his word for it — until the trial at least.'

'I see. The very well-respected town drunk.' Holly knew that Tukwa would never live to see any trial.

'He's respectable enough when he's sober.' Creelock shrugged. He stepped clear of the shadows and called to his men to stop shooting, before shouting towards the stables, 'All right, you Paiute scum, you better come on out now. You ain't got no chance of shooting your way out of there, so you better just throw your weapons out and follow with your hands held high. No one will open fire on you, you have my word.'

Holly knew that Creelock wanted nothing more than for Tukwa to come out shooting, so he and his men could shoot him down. Why was he so all fired up about killing the Paiute? Had he seen his own death in Tukwa's eyes? Did the massacre of innocent women and children haunt him so much that he recognized bloody vengeance when it came at last?

For a few minutes there was silence on the street. Everyone waited, faces behind windows filled with both fear and morbid interest in what happened next, the regulators tense and ready to shoot down anyone who appeared in the stable doorway, despite Creelock's empty words. Holly dropped his hands to his guns, regretful that the storm had come too soon. More time to find out just what was happening here in Lazarus would have suited him better, and more time to find James and Catherine's killer.

Creelock had just started to shout another warning, when gunshots and the thunder of hoofs drowned his words. The stable doors exploded outwards with the fury of stampeding horseflesh. Everyone who'd been waiting ran in all directions, and somewhere in their rushing midst, as he got himself clear of the oncoming hoofs, Holly glimpsed cavalry trousers and a red headband.

The regulators could only watch in frustration as the largest bunch of horses stampeded past them. Emmett tried for a shot, but nicked a white-nosed mare that reared up in pain and panic, stampeded along the boardwalk, scattering Hobb and Raine from their positions. Hobb ran into the street, to be knocked senseless by galloping horseflesh, while Raine jumped through an open window in a barber shop.

As the dust finally settled, Holly permitted himself a tight grin. 'That was well done, Tukwa,' he whispered to himself. He strolled across the street, passing a moaning Hobb as he slowly came to. 'Maybe they kicked some brains into him,' he said, as he came up on Creelock.

Creelock glared at him, the red eye blazing with anger. 'We'll get him. I'll have my men out after him once they get their horses back.'

'And I'll want a talk with this Henry Potter,' Holly said grimly. 'Once he sobers up enough to string words.'

'This ain't nothing to do with you, Mister Federal Officer,' Creelock snarled. 'It's town business. You ain't talking to no one unless I allow it.'

'Well, I guess you could try stopping me,' Holly said gently, 'and we'll see what happens.' The gentleness failed to reach his frost-cold eyes.

'I got five armed and professional men,' Creelock warned.

'You'll need them, although that one don't look too professional right about now.'

Hobb was sitting in the street, dazed and fumbling around for something he seemed to have lost — his senses perhaps. Several ladies had come to his aid and were attempting to help him up. Holly recognized one of them and went over to her.

'Hello again, Mrs Norton, I see you reached Lazarus without any further mishaps.'

Rachel Norton raised her eyes to the tall marshal and tried to return his smile, but the weary tension in her face weakened it considerably.

'Why Mrs Norton, are you feeling all right?'

Rachel straightened and left Hobb to the other women. Pulling herself together she said, 'All this shooting and . . . yes, I'm fine, Marshal. It's just my nerves. This town is . . . I'm happy to see you, Mr Holly. I'm glad you're here.'

'How are you and your husband doing here, and young Johnny?'

A voice called from across the street. 'Marshal Holly, is that really you?' Harvey Norton was standing in the doorway of his general store, keeping a hold on his son who seemed eager to get into the midst of all the excitement

121

on the street. 'Bring him on in here, Rachel, I got coffee going out back.'

As Harvey vanished into the store Johnny ran over to the marshal. Following Holly and his mother back across the street he gasped out a wide-eyed, breathless story of what he'd seen of the gunplay. Inside, the store was deeply shadowed after the cold, bright sunlight outside, but Holly made out the usual tables displaying clothing, hats, watch-chains, bolts of cloth, tools and basic machinery, and a display case only half filled with pistols. A rack of shotguns and rifles was hung behind the main counter, with drawers for cartridges underneath.

'Johnny, you keep a watch out here,' Rachel ordered the boy. 'Call out if we got any customers.'

'Aw, Ma,' Johnny protested, 'I wanted to ask Holly about — '

'Johnny, you do as I say. And it's 'Mister' Holly to you, young man. You'll have plenty of time to pester the marshal later.'

As Rachel led Holly into a small parlour in back of the store, she said, 'He's still going on about that night on the mountain. He wants to hear about you hunting and killing that man. I've tried telling him that you had no choice, but that it was a terrible thing, but you know what boys are like. You're his hero, Marshal.'

She don't sound too happy about it, Holly thought, but he understood the worries that mothers had over their growing sons well enough. His own mother had seen her sons take to violent professions, and he knew how vexed she'd been at the stories that came back to her of their deeds. The father of Nathan, James and Lisa Holly had been a successful lawyer before his death, and if he'd been unhappy at the way in which his sons chose to enforce the law, he'd never shown it. Edward Holly had been a reserved, stoical gentleman who rarely voiced whatever emotions he might be feeling. He'd died of a cancer that ate him away without his giving much in the way of complaint, and his wife, Abigail, had survived him by only a few years. Only Lisa had been at her deathbed, with her lawyer husband. Holly had always wondered if Lisa's choice of the young lawyer had been influenced by her devotion to her father.

Holly pushed the memory away and took the offered seat at a little table by the window. Harvey sat across from him, while Rachel poured them coffee and then seated herself.

'So how does Lazarus stack up against your expectations?' Holly asked.

The Nortons glanced at each other, and in that glance Holly read their concern. 'It could be all that Lester promised,' Harvey said. 'He has ambitions beyond the silver mining. We got the river down to Logan and we got trees, so there's a logging business waiting for finance. He's taking enough silver out of here already and he's just waiting for the money to start flowing back in. He wants to build a growing, permanent community, and me and Rachel sure want to be a part of it. It could be a good place to bring up children, give them a decent future.'

Holly looked at them both. 'There's a 'but' in there someplace.'

Harvey nodded. 'Since he took on Creelock and them regulators there's been a feeling of unease, like things ain't right no more. It ain't nothing you can put your finger on exactly, since they do keep things peaceful and they've run all the troublemakers out of town. But there's a kind of threat comes off of them, like the stink off a dead polecat, like if you cross one of them, even by accident, you're up against real trouble.'

'Everyone feels it,' Rachel added, 'especially the women. That skinny-faced one with the squint . . . Emmett Marley they call him,' Rachel tried to suppress a shudder at the thought of him and failed, 'he likes the ladies, if I can put it so delicately. The dentist's wife, Emma Whatley, says he cornered her in an alleyway a few days back and she feared for her virtue until Harvey here happened by. The few boys we have in town have taken to tormenting them, and I'm afraid of them going too far and what might happen. I had to take a catapult off Johnny just the other day. He was up on the roof of the bank, that unfinished building by the saloon, shooting at two of Creelock's men. If I hadn't seen what was happening, I don't know what they might have done. Emmett is a favourite target, it seems.'

'I met up with Emmett Marley last evening,' Holly told them. 'His winning personality got lost on me, I have to confess. We had a bit of a disagreement.'

Harvey looked alarmed. 'Be careful around them, Marshal. They're dangerous men.'

'I have a reputation in that direction myself. How is your business doing? Shona says the miners ain't been paid in a while.' In answer to Rachel's raising of a questioning eyebrow, he added,

'Shona Gordillo and I are old friends. You could say we've covered a lot of ground and seen a lot of towns together.'

'Shona has been a good friend to us as well,' Harvey said, giving his wife a warning look not to enquire further into the marshal's relationship with Shona Gordillo. 'Business is slow, but only because the miners are waiting to be paid. We got a lot of merchandise going out on promissory notes. There's to be a big delivery of funds up to the mine in the next few days.'

Holly's interest was instantly aroused. 'How is it being delivered?'

'That we don't know. Lester is playing it close to the vest, keeping the actual method of delivery a secret.'

'That sounds like good sense. I asked Shona and now I'm asking you if you know of anyone missing from the town or the mine?' Harvey shrugged his ignorance and asked why. 'There was a body found a few miles outside of town, frozen solid and half-eaten.'

'Half-eaten!' Johnny exclaimed. He'd been listening at the door. 'You mean it was eaten by wolves?'

While Rachel scolded her son and Harvey went to check whether there were customers waiting, Holly took his leave. Figuring it was time he paid a visit to Lester Ryle, he headed down to the stables. A couple of runaway horses were being led back to their stalls as he entered. He was saddling his pinto, the only mount not stampeded by Tukwa, when a shadow fell across the bright square of sunlight from the open doors.

Holly swung around, his Colt already clear of its holster and taking deadly aim at the boy who stood there — Billy Dill's eyes widened in alarm.

'What are you doing creeping up behind me?' Holly demanded. 'Open your coat, slow and careful, and then get your hands up real high.'

The boy's fingers shook as he unbuttoned his plaid coat, holding it wide. Nothing but a rough shirt and braces underneath, but Holly lifted the coat and checked all around for any weapons tucked in the back of his britches. Finding nothing he motioned for the boy to drop his arms. He looked keenly at the youth's clear, unblemished features. If it wasn't for the vacant, slightly confused look in the blue eyes, and the slackness of the mouth, Billy Dill would be a right handsome young man. Handsome enough to be the man Sarah Fennell had told him about. He had fair skin and corn-coloured hair. It wasn't shoulder length like Sarah had said, but hair was easily cut.

Undecided whether Billy Dill was putting on the simple act or not, Holly barked, 'What do you want here, boy?'

Billy swallowed nervously, and then said, 'Miss Shona, she said to tell you that the gambler man was asking about you this morning. Danielle told him who you were and he lit out right after.'

Well, that's right interesting, Holly thought. It could mean he's the man I'm looking for, or it could be that he had an urgent appointment somewhere.

It looks like I got two suspects and no clear idea which one is Jack Weaver, if it's either one of them.

Before leaving for the mine he took a turn around the streets, familiarizing himself with the layout. It didn't take long, as the fledgling community hadn't yet grown by much. He stopped by the skeletal wooden building on the edge of town, where a young bearded man was lighting the lantern hanging over the doorless opening.

'Seems like a waste of time,' Holly said. 'It's broad daylight and this ain't proper built yet.'

The young man turned towards him and Holly took in the dog-collar and the hazel eyes. So, it was a church then. And he's not Jack Weaver, Holly reckoned, thankful that no more suspects were piling up.

'Reverend Mathew Ellis,' the man introduced himself, offering his hand up to the still mounted Holly. 'The lantern stays lit day and night. The church might not be finished, but the light will burn here. All who need guidance will know where to find it,' he cast a glance at the nearby jailhouse, 'although those who need it most are unlikely to seek it out. But that was ever the challenge, was it not?'

'I reckon so,' Holly agreed, unsure if he was included in that unenlightened company.

He talked to the reverend for a few more minutes, deciding he liked the earnest young man. As he headed up into the hills a swirl of snow swept in, thin but still chilling on exposed skin. Holly pulled the collar of the sheepskin coat higher and fixed the bandanna up over his face. The trail had been beaten down by heavy wagons and much use over recent months, and Holly rode at an easy pace.

10

The Lazarus Mining Company

Holly had seen mining camps before, but this one seemed busier and more prosperous than most, although the older workings still lay rusting and unused alongside the new. Cars ran on multiple tracks in and out of the wide, rough-hewn mine entrance, beehive shaped lime kilns dotted the site and an aerial tramway delivered ore to a stone mill high on the hillside, its tall chimney overlooking the bustling industry going on below. Scores of workers hurried about above ground.

There were numerous tents and cabins erected on the road in, with a much larger blockhouse raised up on a broad rock table above the site. Constructed using massive logs, it looked solid and permanent, and was reached by a steep staircase that wound its way up the rock face. Smoke drifted from a massive stone chimney rising through the centre of the building. Holly could see figures moving behind a large central window. Wooden flaps with firing slits cut in them could easily be dropped in case of attack. As a defensive strong point it was well positioned, and probably a wise decision in this wilderness — you could never be sure what might come against you. This Lester Ryle was nobody's fool, and that was for sure.

'What's your business here, mister?'

It was the same sort of greeting Holly had received when arriving in the town, and the same sort of hardcase who delivered it. Holly's eyes passed over the sallow-faced man, well muffled in a heavy, ankle-length coat and thick comforter, to the cabin he'd stepped out of. Another man stood in the doorway, a rifle cradled in his arms and his eyes watchful of the newcomer's intent. He was a massive black man;

about six five, Holly reckoned, and clearly another one of Creelock's regulators, as was the man who'd stepped into the road ahead of him.

'I'm here to see Mr Lester Ryle, the boss of this outfit.'

'What's your business with Mr Ryle?'

'That's for his ears alone.'

The man started to raise his rifle, motioning to the black man to do the same. He stopped when Holly pulled his coat back and displayed the marshal's badge on his vest. 'My name is Nathan Holly. I'm a federal officer. I already had a talk with your boss back in Lazarus.'

The man lowered his rifle. 'Just doing my job, Marshal.'

'You'd be LaVey and Ponder I guess.'

The man nodded. 'I'm Lamar LaVey, and that there's Zach Ponder.' He pointed towards the blockhouse. 'Mr Ryle is up there. That's his office and living-quarters. I seen him go up a few minutes ago.'

Holly thanked him and urged the

pinto over to the wooden staircase. The steep climb winded him some and he reflected that he was getting too old for this sort of thing. But then, what else would he do? He'd been a lawman half his life, and unless he found a fortune hidden away someplace and settled down with Shona Gordillo, he reckoned he'd die as one.

The cabin door opened just as he reached it, and a man who was about to step through jerked backwards at the sight of him, sudden alarm flashing in his eyes. After a moment he regained his composure and said, 'I'm so sorry, you startled me.' He studied the stranger for a second before saying, 'I don't know you, do I? You're not employed here.'

Holly introduced himself and the man said, 'Do come on in, Marshal. I apologize once more. We don't see many strangers around here, especially up here at the mine. My name is McQueen, Warren McQueen. I'm Mr Ryle's legal adviser and accountant, amongst other things.'

The man was stooped over, scarecrow thin, with grey, waxy-looking skin and a prematurely bald pate for someone who looked to be under thirty. He had a scratchy little beard, the hair so fine and pale it was hardly worth the growing. He looked ill, his blue eyes weak and watery. As he led Holly inside a racking cough doubled him over.

'I'm all right,' he gasped as Holly put out a hand to steady him. 'Quite all right, no need to concern yourself.'

The spacious office was littered with tables, desks and notice-boards; oil lamps hung or settled close to where men were working, and a huge safe stuffed with papers lay gaping open against one wall. Holly noted that there was no money stashed amongst the papers. A heavyset man with mutton-chop whiskers, luxuriant moustaches, and with a pair of small round glasses perched on the tip of his nose, was bent over a chart with two others, clearly his clerks from what Holly heard.

'I think closing that particular shaft might be wise, allow us to concentrate our efforts elsewhere.' He looked up and saw McQueen with a stranger. Once McQueen had made the introductions, Ryle beamed at the marshal and said, 'I heard how you helped the Nortons on their way up here. Bully for you, sir. I admire a man of courage who'll come to the aid of their fellows when danger threatens. What can I do for you, sir, and what say we indulge in some hot coffee while we talk?'

Holly liked the man on instinct. He was a bluff, honest sort who crackled with energy, intelligence and humour in equal measures. It was no surprise to Holly, now that he'd met him, that Lester Ryle had enough faith in his own abilities to attempt the building of an entire community, or to believe that others would follow him. If anyone could do it, this man surely could.

McQueen joined them at Ryle's insistence and the three went through into a parlour just off a kitchen area.

Once Holly had told his story, Ryle sat back in his chair, his sorrowful eyes surveying the marshal from behind his round little glasses. 'You have my sympathies, Marshal. You must grieve terribly for your brother, and anyone who harms a lady is just the lowest form of life. I'll surely help you in any way that is at all possible.'

'You killed all four of those men?' McQueen said. He'd been shocked and horrified when hearing about the fight in Logan, and it clearly hadn't worn off.

Holly ignored him, addressing Ryle instead. 'First thing I have to ask is if you seen any strangers around, in particular one with long fair hair, blue eyes, handsome-looking and with charm to spare for the ladies? The second thing is if you got anyone missing up at the mine here?'

Ryle exchanged a worried look with McQueen. 'Why yes, as a matter of fact one of our clerks disappeared a few days ago. His name was Edgar Pullman, a young fellow out of New York. A sensitive sort, I was a mite concerned about hiring him, and I was proved right. He never took to life up here, became quite sickly and morose. We thought he might have just lit out back to civilization. What do you know of him, Marshal?'

'Well, I can't say for sure it's your missing clerk, but I found a body not far from town, frozen and half eaten by wolves. Whoever he was he didn't suffer no accident; he was killed, by person or persons unknown.'

Ryle's eyes behind the glasses widened in horror and complete bafflement. 'But who would want to kill Edgar? He had no money — no one has been paid in a while — and I can't imagine he'd give offence to anyone.'

'What did he do for you up here, Mr Ryle?'

It was McQueen who answered. 'He was in charge of the stores, kept a check on the provisions, tools and equipment, made sure everything was accounted for and nothing went missing. You know what it's like with an operation this size.'

Holly grunted. 'And nothing has gone missing?'

'No, Edgar was very good at his job.'

'Warren knew him back East,' Ryle added. 'He knew he had a good reputation.'

At that moment a vision in a powder-blue dress swept into the parlour and threw her arms around McQueen. 'Warren dearest, I've had food on the table this last twenty minutes or more. I sent one of the men to fetch you and now I find you still here. You need to eat regular if you're to get your strength back.'

Holly stood up. 'I'm afraid that was my fault. I arrived just as Mr McQueen was leaving and delayed him with some questions.'

'Marshal Holly, this is Laura McQueen, Warren's lovely wife.' Ryle beamed. 'Laura, the marshal has some disturbing news concerning our missing clerk.'

'You mean poor Edgar? What's happened to him?' Laura McQueen's green eyes flashed with alarm, an effect that did nothing but add to their prettiness.

While Ryle and her husband told her about the body by the river, Holly took the opportunity to admire Laura McQueen. She was a fine-looking lady, with golden-blonde hair that fell in curled ringlets, long dark eyelashes, and attractively gentle curves under the fetching blue dress — although the dress did seem a mite lacking in material for the cold mountain air. Once they'd finished talking she asked the marshal directly if he thought it was Edgar Pullman's corpse.

'Well, I need someone who knew him to come into town and make the identification. The face is gone but the clothing might give a clue. But, in the meantime, I don't want to delay your husband's meal a moment longer, Mrs McQueen.' He turned to Warren. 'You best cut along with your wife before I get into any more trouble.'

'I'll come into town tomorrow, Marshal,' McQueen said. 'I reckon I knew Edgar better than anyone, so I'll make the identification. I'm praying it isn't him, but we'll know tomorrow.'

Laura McQueen led her husband out, telling him to mind the stairs. 'We have to take care' were the last words Holly heard as they made their way down. It was obvious the woman fretted over her husband's condition, whatever it was.

'What's wrong with him?' the marshal asked. 'He looks like a stiff wind might knock him over.'

'Consumption would be my guess. If it is I reckon the mountain air might do him good. They don't really talk about it, and it wasn't mentioned in his letters when accepting the job. He was delayed getting here. I expected him a few weeks earlier, but from what Laura told me he was unable to travel.'

'You never met him before he came up here?'

'I knew of him from a mutual acquaintance; my lawyer and sort of roving agent, Tom Loomis. He does a

142

lot of recruiting for me, and he'd worked with Warren before, in one of those big legal firms in New York specializing in financial matters. Warren and I corresponded by mail. I was surprised when he accepted my offer of a position here. Double surprised when he turned up with a young wife in tow. But he said they both found it right desirable to be in on the start of such a large enterprise. He seems to have a lot of faith in my ambitions for this place.'

'I find it curious that you've invested so much in silver mining,' Holly admitted. 'I thought that the fourth coinage act a few years ago put all you boys out of business.'

'Ah yes, the crime of '73; it did a lot of damage, I'll admit. When they demonetized silver and adopted gold as the only metallic standard they destroyed a lot of big interests. There's a lot of pressure on the treasury though, from some very powerful people, and I have faith that they're going to be buying silver again very soon, and at a high price.

There'll always be a market, however, if you look for it. It's a gamble, I'll admit, but it's not my only card for building a permanent community here.'

'You're talking about logging?'

'Indeed. We have the Marys River and we have the timber in plentiful supply. My intent is to have a railway spur up to Lazarus pretty soon. We're already building a bank, a church and a school. At the moment some of the women are teaching school in the back of the Norton store. Rachel Norton got them organized. We already got a telegraph office up and running.'

The mention of a bank got Holly thinking. 'You say no one's been paid in a while, and they were saying as much in town. What's the problem?'

Ryle sighed. 'We got the money — that's not the problem — it's just getting such large amounts moved from my backers to the bank in Logan and then up to us here in the wilderness. But it's coming up tomorrow, and it'll be a relief to us all, mine workers and townsfolk alike.'

Holly knew who was bringing it. 'Sam Sugar. He said he'd be up here in a couple of days.'

'That's right; Marshal Sugar is bringing it up in supply wagons, but wagons protected by him and four of his deputies. Tom Loomis is down there right now getting it organized. Half the money will be deposited in the bank in Logan until we get our own bank up and running, the rest will come up here to get everyone paid. Creelock and his deputies are on watch as well. It'll be the first time I've felt they're worth their pay, although they did rid the town of a few troublemakers.'

Figuring as how he had some things to think on, Holly took his leave. As Ryle escorted him out of the blockhouse, it was to a darkening sky and thickening snowfall. Climbing down the first flight of stairs, Holly had a thought and called back to Ryle before he could disappear inside. 'Who hired Creelock and his men?'

'They were recommended to Warren as peacekeepers for hire. Who recommended them I don't know, but I checked on them and they have worked in other towns and for a couple of the big ranch owners. Creelock and Zach Ponder down there, they were both army men, served with distinction as far as I know. But the thing is that they were dealing with pretty violent situations in the army, and then with dangerous rustling outfits for the ranches. From things I've been hearing I feel they're a mite too rough for the folks in Lazarus. Once this current situation is resolved I'll be cutting them loose and appointing a town marshal.'

'A wise decision I think. And this man I'm looking for, you have no sighting of such a person among your people?'

Ryle shook his head and promised to ask around.

Holly took the rough trail back down the mountain, the snow coming at him in frenzied gusts, half blinding him. He had covered only a few miles before he was sure he was being shadowed. There was an uncomfortable itch in his back, like it had become a target, nicely centred in someone's gunsights.

11

Curtain of White, Game of Death

Holly reined in on a snow-covered bluff. Rising in the saddle he gazed down over the canyon below. The river, heavy with ice, moved sluggish and dark as it snaked close to the eastern side, where huge broken boulders lay jumbled against a sheer rock wall. He'd passed this way on the journey up, and had stopped by the river. His memory of a certain place in the canyon was confirmed by what he saw. His back still itching, he rode down and dismounted.

Kneeling by the river, making it look like he was filling his canteen, he listened intently, kept a watch on his back trail, and sniffed at the frost-laden air. He was offering his stalker an easy, sitting target to tempt him out from cover. With his back to the rock wall an attack had to come from the front or the sides. The thick, swirling flakes of snow were in his favour, but it was still risky just sitting there: riskier still on the trail, though, when a bullet could come at any time and from any direction. Behind him there was a fissure in one of the massive boulders that lay tight to the cliff wall; from a distance it looked as if that was all it was, but Holly knew different. He'd seen a mule deer emerge from it on the trip up and had found a steep, narrow incline hidden behind the fissure that led to a rock ledge higher up and a distance away, screened by rock and brushwood.

If he could just tempt his mysterious foe out from cover it might give him the edge he needed.

Who in hell is it anyway, he wondered; someone from the mine workings? One of the two regulators, perhaps, but he didn't figure on Creelock having had enough time to order him to be either followed or ambushed. The best chance for survival was to assume an intended ambush, and that he was engaged in a game of life or death.

It was faint but Holly heard it — the snap of a twig and a bullet being levered into a rifle. He rolled backwards as the shot echoed around the valley and snow and stone chips flew up in a cloud, just inches away from him. He crabbed back into the shadowed cleft, as more bullets hammered against the rock. He fired a couple of random shots back, but for show only, before moving back through the narrow fissure and out on to the incline. The shooting had stopped, and he could almost read his attacker's thoughts. Thinking he had his prey trapped in a crack in the rock, he'd be moving position to put a few slugs right into the depths of the shadowy recess.

Holly climbed quickly. Halfway up he lost his footing on the steep incline and sent a shower of small stones back down the slope. He lay prone for a few minutes, hardly breathing, waiting for the hail of lead that would tell him the fall had been heard. When nothing happened he moved on, finally stopping on the rock ledge, about forty feet north of his previous position, and thirty feet higher up. Lying prone, he peered down through the curtain of thick white drifting flakes, just about making out a blurry figure on the far bank of the river. The heavy snowfall was an enemy to them both now. The man was inching towards the river, breaking cover completely as he took aim towards the rock fissure, but the snow made him indistinct, hiding him completely for seconds at a time.

'Just give me one clear shot,' Holly muttered. He would have preferred that his shadower were taken alive and questioned, but the situation didn't allow much in the way of choices.

Figuring he was in position the shadower began blasting away, the gun flashes lighting up the snow curtain and giving Holly a better target. He shouldered the Winchester and loosed off three shots in rapid succession. He saw the man fall, but couldn't know if it was fatal as the white curtain closed in around them again.

Holly waited and watched for any movement. Remembering Teague's deception that had almost succeeded in killing him, he was reluctant to go down and check his accuracy. He was just about to move when muffled hoof-beats from the valley floor stopped him.

A rider on the far side of the river reined in opposite the rock fissure. Dismounting, he knelt over the fallen man, and then raised his face to the far cliff-face. He stood and waved both arms, and Holly saw that it was Tukwa, who was telling him his mysterious attacker was dead.

Joining him on the far bank, Holly looked at the dead gambler. 'Nevins. Well, I guess that answers the question of who 'Jack Weaver' really was. He had no cause to come at me unless he knew

I was after him, and he fits the description, just a little shabbier than I expected. He was the last man, Tukwa. I guess I got them all.'

The Paiute gave him a solemn look. 'You got revenge for your family.'

Holly shook his head. 'I got justice, Tukwa, but I'd have preferred to see him judged and hanged. This was more merciful than a rope, and I didn't owe him no mercy.'

'I will show no mercy when I kill Creelock,' Tukwa said. 'I did not steal any horses, Marshal.'

'I never thought you did. Creelock either recognized you or his conscience has him jumping at Paiute ghosts. After what he did, he's maybe been waiting for someone like you to find him.'

'And I have found him.'

'Just don't be making your move until we have some chance of winning,' Holly cautioned. 'There's something going on here that don't smell right. I got to figure it out, and maybe change the odds in our favour. Where have you been hiding out?'

'I circled back into town, looking for you. Your friend, Miss Shona, told that boy who works for her to show me a place in the hills, old mine workings with a cabin.'

'Billy Dill, I owe him an apology. You stay hid there, and when the time is right I'll send Billy for you.'

Tukwa grunted. 'I will stay hidden, but not for long. Creelock will not escape me again. I will see he dies screaming.'

'It won't be for long,' Holly said grimly. 'Whatever's going to happen, it'll be soon, and I got a feeling in my bones that it'll be bloody.'

★ ★ ★

Lazarus was quiet when Holly rode in near sundown. The few streetlamps already installed threw pools of warm yellow light over the newly fallen snow. It had slowed some as Holly rode down off the mountain and now only stray flakes drifted across the main street as he paid a visit to the telegraph office, and then tethered the pinto outside the regulators' building. None of Creelock's men were about, and the marshal let himself in, walking quietly across the entrance hall to the office.

Creelock was alone, sitting hunched by the foul-smelling fire, a single lamp lit on the desk. An open book lay by him on the floor, and to Holly's astonishment the man's shoulders were shaking.

'Creelock?'

The shoulders stilled, but it took a few moments before the man turned. He'd been dabbing at his eyes, but Holly saw the liquid gaze and the stained cheeks. The red eye looked ghastly, as though watery blood seeped from its infernal depths. Holly could only stare at him until he spoke.

'I must apologize, Marshal.' The rasping voice was thick with emotion and he dabbed at the scarlet orb once more. 'I would spare us both any embarrassment, but Mister Dickens does not permit it.' He waved a hand at the book on the floor. 'You see, young Nell has died and her grandfather sits by her grave, awaiting her return. I fear, however, that she is gone for ever, that poor sweet child.'

'Resurrection is a trick most find difficult to pull off,' Holly told him gruffly. 'I guess I should have announced myself, so I'm sorry to intrude on a private moment, but I got a corpse outside, bleeding all over my rig.'

The eyes opened fully and glistened in the firelight. 'Another dead body — are we to expect similar offerings every time you ride into town, Marshal? The graveyard in Lazarus will be filling much faster than we reckoned on.'

'The difference is that I know who this one is. He's a gambler called Nevins, also called Jack Weaver, and probably a mess of other names as well. He tried to shoot me down on the trail, but neither his luck nor his skill was up to it.'

'Then I guess he's the man you came looking for. That means you'll be leaving us. I can't say I'm sorry. The population might decrease a little less rapidly.'

'I'll be leaving in my own good time,' Holly growled. 'I have Warren McQueen coming in tomorrow to identify the other corpse. He thinks it might be a man called Edgar Pullman, a clerk up at the mine. Do you know him?'

'Never met him, but this isn't your concern, Holly. This is town business, and that makes it my concern.'

'Why do you think he was killed, Creelock?'

'I have no idea, and I guess you don't either. A lover's quarrel, a jealous rival, someone he cheated, or perhaps just a simple robbery; there's lots of reasons why people get themselves killed.'

'There's one you haven't mentioned. Maybe it was because of his job.'

Holly saw the barb hit home. For just a moment Creelock betrayed his alarm, and then his face settled into a cold mask, determined to give nothing more away. 'You really should back off,

Marshal,' he advised. 'Leave it alone when it don't concern you.'

'Backing off is something I never learned.'

Creelock nodded. 'I heard that about you,' he allowed.

Holly couldn't leave him without one more jibe. 'You know, Creelock, you came up here with great expectations, but I got a feeling you're about to hit on hard times.'

Heading over to the Silver Palace, after disposing of the gambler's body with the town undertaker, Holly was still chuckling to himself over Creelock's discomfiture. Emmett Marley was standing on the boardwalk outside the Palace, watching him come with an aggrieved air. Holly was nearly up on him when he heard the soft whoosh of some small object flying through the air, followed by a sharp thud. Emmett yelped in pain and two giggling boys ran down the alleyway between the Palace and the unfinished bank. One of them was Johnny Norton.

Rubbing at his rear, Emmett was about to give chase when Holly stepped in his path. 'They're just boys, Emmett. Let them go.'

'Like hell I will. They're always at that. I had enough.'

He tried to push past the marshal, but Holly stood his ground. 'I'll talk to the mothers and we'll get those catapults off them.'

Emmett wasn't having it. He swung at Holly, missed, and got a short right to the ribs in return. Holly's big fist had an impact like solid stone. Gasping and wheezing, Emmett sat down on the boardwalk outside the Palace, but as Holly stepped up past him he pulled his sidearm.

'Emmett! Don't do it!' Creelock called from across the street. 'He'll kill you for sure.'

'Good advice,' Holly agreed, giving Emmett a hard stare.

Emmett pushed the pistol back in his holster and staggered over to his boss, clutching painfully at his ribs and rubbing at his rear.

One of Shona's girls, the dark and slender Danielle, appeared in the doorway of the Palace. 'Nathan Holly, are you making trouble again?'

'Not by myself. Young Johnny Norton and his pal were doing their share.'

He looked towards the alleyway, but the boys were gone. He'd have to talk to the parents. Emmett Marley was way too volatile for them to be taking such risks. Especially since this particular game of death was just getting started.

12

Dynamite Man

It was past four in the morning, but Holly couldn't sleep. He heaved up out of bed, trying not to awaken the sleeping Shona. Pulling a chair over by the window he looked down on the sleeping town of Lazarus. It had been another quiet evening, but from what Lester Ryle had said about the delivery Sam Sugar was bringing in, tomorrow night would see wild celebrations rock the town.

Holly allowed his gaze to drift over the snow-covered street to where Creelock and his men awaited tomorrow's long anticipated payday. He thought about all he'd seen and heard since arriving, and what he'd been told by Spanish Jack just moments before he died, and he tried putting it all together.

Jack Weaver — Nevins — had had a big job lined up in Lazarus, and it was easy to see what it was. It was a job he couldn't do alone, not with Sam Sugar and his men protecting the payroll. Speck had said the bank in Stillwater had been done for travelling money, but it was more than that. Weaver needed the money to buy Creelock and his men. He'd needed as many guns as he could get, he'd even offered Speck a place in the gang. Were Speck, Shilto, Broome and Hinks supposed to become four more regulators, or just drifters stopping over in Lazarus? Were they along as insurance, in case of a double-cross from Creelock?

Speck hadn't known what the job was, and Holly wondered how many of the bunch who'd been riding with Weaver knew what he had planned. Holly's instincts told him none of them.

And what about Creelock; did he know what was coming in on the supply wagons? Did he know the plan? Was he simply paid to stay out of any play

Weaver and his men made, or was he hired to deal with any opposition from Sugar's men? Creelock was nobody's fool, and he must have guessed what Weaver's target was. Weaver couldn't have been that sure of Creelock, so maybe he'd needed his own gang so the regulators didn't cut him out once they had the strongboxes. But with his men all killed by Holly, Weaver was left with just the regulators. However it had played, even with Weaver himself amongst the dead, the plan, whatever it was, was about to go ahead. What Holly couldn't figure was how they were going to stop the townsfolk, or even any mine workers who might be in town, from getting in the fight on Sam Sugar's side. It was their payroll that was at stake, after all.

Holly considered Captain Joshua Creelock a man who could shed tears over the death of a fictional young girl, and yet sleep nights after murdering women and children. Even in such a man, lacking mercy or conscience, there was some morsel of humanity hiding itself away. Of course, Nell hadn't been a Paiute, and maybe that made all the difference to a man like Creelock.

Holly's thoughts turned to Creelock's presence in Lazarus, which must have seemed to Weaver, once he was able to bribe him, a stroke of amazing good fortune. Or was it? How had Weaver even known about Lazarus, and about the problems Lester Ryle was having with the movement of large sums of money? He must have planned all this months ago, so he'd known the bank wasn't built and that payrolls were delivered at lengthy intervals, and that consequently they were very large when they did occur.

Holly stared into the blue-tinged darkness as sleep finally descended on him. Voices came at him and images flashed before him as consciousness faded — James's letter and Catherine's eyes glittering like precious gems; a pitted rock surface stained with blood, clothing wedged in between the cracks, hair the colour of spun gold and matted with gore, Sarah Fennell's swooning over Nevins — or was it Jack Weaver? The river surged up, a frozen corpse tossed on the black, ice-covered turbulence, face half-eaten. It changed, became the accountant's face, frozen in shock at the sight of a stranger. A woman's voice saying, 'We have to take care.'

The voices and images faded away as Holly sank into a troubled sleep.

* * *

Shona either believed in a large breakfast or she figured Holly needed a lot of feeding up to maintain that massive frame. Holly stared in disbelief at the heaped plates of bacon, eggs and ham that Lucy was laying in front of him and the boss.

'Shona, if I eat all of that I won't be able to get out from under this table.' He looked to Lucy for some guidance on the matter. 'Does she normally breakfast like this?'

Lucy shot her employer a wicked grin as she poured coffee for them both. 'It depends on how much of a workout she's had the night before.'

'Thank you, Lucy,' Shona said primly. 'That will be all. We can manage the rest by ourselves.'

'Oh, I'm quite sure of that,' Lucy laughed, hurrying out of range of her employer's attempted swat.

'That girl needs her bottom tanned,' Shona said. 'Danielle is the same. They never show the proper respect.'

Holly grinned. 'They love you a lot, Shona. Loyalty like that can't ever be bought.'

They were halfway through the mountain of food when Billy Dill came in, approaching Holly with round and frightened eyes.

Holly felt a surge of regret over his earlier actions. 'It's all right, Billy,' he said gently. 'I apologize for my behaviour yesterday. I know you're a good, honest boy now and I won't never scare

166

you like that again, I promise. What have you got there? Is that for me, from the telegraph office?'

Billy gave him a nervous smile and handed him the folded paper. While he read, Shona asked furiously, 'What did you do to scare him? I heard nothing about this. Billy, what did this big buffalo do to you? Nathan?' Nathan's deep silence and hardened expression as he read stopped her. 'Nathan? What is that?'

He looked up at her. 'It's information from the army on two ex-soldiers. There's no mention of Creelock hitting the wrong band of Paiute and murdering women and children, as you'd expect. Just an honourable discharge, which means they hushed it up. Zach Ponder was a sergeant who served under Creelock. He was also a dynamite man. His area of expertise was explosives.'

'That means something to you?'

'It does. It means I know why Edgar Pullman was killed, and how they intend making sure that hundreds of

167

mine workers and townsfolk don't interfere with the robbery.'

'Robbery?' Shona spluttered. 'What robbery? You don't mean — hell, it's coming up here today, isn't it? It'll be here by noon. It isn't just supplies that Sugar's bringing. They're going to take the payroll.'

Holly pushed his chair back. 'I got to see Harvey Norton. Billy, I need you to go find Tukwa up at that shack, tell him it's going to happen around noon.' He gave Shona a rough, bearlike hug that squeezed the breath from her and headed out into the street, where the first thing he saw was Warren McQueen and his wife coming down main street, with Laura, not her husband, taking the reins of a rather old and battered-looking horse-drawn surrey. Holly reckoned the rough trail might have proved too much for the frail-looking Warren.

Seeing the marshal, Warren called out, 'We came to look at your corpse, Marshal. If it is Edgar, my wife wanted to pay her respects.'

168

'He's over with the undertaker. I got some business, but I'll catch up to you later,' Holly said, his gaze passing over the two horses tethered behind the surrey.

Seeing his interest, Laura said quickly, 'They need fresh shod. We're leaving them with the blacksmith.'

Holly nodded and bid them good day, saying once more that he'd catch up to them later. As he crossed the street he saw Lamar LaVey riding in. They were all gathering. Only Zach Ponder was left up at the mine, and Holly knew why. He went into the Nortons' store and found Rachel demanding that her son must turn over his weapon.

'Aw Ma, we wasn't going to shoot at Emmett no more, honest we wasn't.'

'Hand it over, young man, right his minute.'

With slow, bitter reluctance, Johnny handed over a roughly fashioned, but highly effective catapult. Rachel shoved it into one of her voluminous skirt pockets and shooed her son outside.

'That boy don't know the trouble he could bring down on himself,' she said to Holly. 'I wouldn't trust one of them regulators not to shoot at a child if the notion took them. Are you looking to buy, Marshal, or are you looking for Harvey?'

Before Holly could reply, Harvey stepped out of the back room.

Holly told him what he needed, and minutes later Harvey was riding out of town towards the mine.

Over on the boardwalk of the Silver Palace, Emmett Marley finished rolling himself a cigarette. He watched Harvey go, and a sly smile touched his lips.

His time was coming, very soon now. He licked the paper, sealing it around the layer of tobacco before placing it between his lips.

As Holly came out of the store and walked towards the undertaker's, Emmett's smile twisted itself even more around his cigarette. 'You're heading in the right direction, Marshal,' he muttered to himself.

He struck a match against his boot heel and as the paper flamed up he watched Holly step through the door, to where Walt Raine and Isiah Hobb were waiting with guns drawn.

13

Johnny Got a Gun

They disarmed Holly and marched him down to the jailhouse. Creelock was sitting with his feet up on his desk as they led the marshal up the stairs and along a corridor that ran the length of the building, windows at both ends. The rooms on the street side were basic bedrooms, with bunk-beds, dressers and washbasins visible, but on the two rooms opposite the doors had been removed and cell doors installed in their place. The windows had bars over them. Only the nearest cell was occupied, by a rumpled man with a bowler-hat over his face. The hat lifted in time with his snores. A tray with an empty plate and a half-filled coffee cup sat outside the cell.

'Your witness, I presume,' Holly said,

as the door of the furthest cell clanged shut on him.

Raine and Hobb ignored him, but Emmett, who had followed them in, gave him a wide grin. 'Why, Mr Potter is all the witness we need, Marshal. A fine upstanding citizen, when he can stand. He seen that Paiute trash stealing horses from the good folk of Lazarus, and then he seen you with him in back of the town, helping a fugitive escape the law. We got no other choice but to lock you up.' He turned to look in at the sleeping Potter. 'Ain't that right, Potter? You'll just swear to that in court, won't you now?'

When Potter didn't respond Emmett tossed the coffee cup into the cell. It bounced off the bowler-hat, splashing its contents over the sleeping man's clothes, but the snoring continued, not missing a beat.

'We had to bring him in again last night,' Emmett chuckled. 'He was getting all rowdy over in the Silver Palace.'

173

Once the cell door was locked, Hobb went back downstairs and Raine settled himself in a chair at the far end of the corridor, close to Holly's cell. Emmett decided to taunt the marshal some more. 'Well, I guess you know why you're really here.' He grinned.

'I know why I'm here,' Holly said.

'Of course you know,' Creelock rasped as he stepped on to the upper floor. His army greatcoat was about his shoulders and a sabre hung by his side; his hat was tilted at a rakish angle above the flowing white hair; every inch the cavalry officer once more. 'I figure you've worked most of it out by now and you know what's about to happen. And you know I have to stop you from taking any action. I can't be taking any chances with a man like you, Marshal.'

'So why didn't your men just shoot me dead?'

'Too soon, Marshal, too soon. We don't want no upset just yet. Sugar and his men won't get here until noon, and by then the town will be cleared. After that, it won't matter how much shooting anyone hears.'

At the thought of Holly's death, Creelock's thin mouth twisted into a cruel smile. With his long white hair and scar, and that blood-red eye, he resembled some bloodthirsty hobgoblin thinking on treats to come. He turned and tramped back down the stairs, his boot heels pounding out a death dirge for the marshal.

★ ★ ★

Shortly before eleven the grumble of distant thunder roused the citizens of Lazarus from their daily round. The sky was clear and bright, and the sound wasn't repeated.

'That didn't seem like thunder to me,' the livery man said.

Coming out on to the street, the undertaker sniffed the air. 'More like an explosion, up at the mine most like.' His instincts about such matters were always sound, his profession perhaps sharpening his senses regarding death and disaster.

Only a short time later the rider came galloping in, telling of explosions and cave-ins and miners trapped underground. They needed every able-bodied man and woman to help care for the injured. In a half hour the town was almost emptied, but not completely.

In the stockroom at the rear of her store, Rachel Norton backed away from Emmett Marley with panic and fear in her eyes. They were emotions Emmett desired to see in his victims, and they acted as a spur to his passions. He bore long scratches on his cheek, where Rachel's nails had raked him. It hadn't been enough to stop him, and he advanced on her again, trapping her against stacked bags of dry goods at the rear of the storeroom.

'There ain't no one left in town but you and me,' he said hoarsely. 'No one's going to spoil our fun, so you'd do better to just relax and enjoy it. It's going to happen anyways, lady; ain't nothing going to stop old Emmett from showing you a real good time.'

Rachel's gaze caught a movement behind him and she shouted, 'No! Johnny, don't!'

The explosion knocked the boy off his feet, and the .44 calibre bullet from the Smith & Wesson model 13 single-action revolver slapped into Emmett's calf and through to the other side, expending its remaining energy into the stockroom floor. Emmett screamed, long and loud, before staggering back against some shelving and pulling his pistol.

It was the pure instinct to protect her son that caused Rachel to fly at the wounded man, bringing him to the ground with herself on top. Johnny, looking terrified by his own actions, scrambled to his feet and joined in. When Creelock entered he was on the floor beside the struggling Emmett and his mother, punching at Emmett's head.

'What in hell?' Creelock yelled. Hobb was with him, and he pulled the boy off. 'Get up off the floor, the both of you. What's going on here? I said no shooting until Sugar arrives.'

'The brat shot a hole in me,' Emmett whined, pointing to the blood flowing from his calf.

Rachel pulled herself off him and stood, shakily dusting herself down. 'My son was protecting me. This animal attacked me.'

Creelock lifted the gun Johnny had dropped. 'Where did this come from?'

'It's one we have on display in the store. Johnny must have loaded it.'

'He shot me,' Emmett continued to whine. 'Little brat shot me.'

'Shut up!' Creelock barked. 'You're lucky he didn't load one of the Greeners, you wouldn't have no leg left. Get them all over to the jailhouse,' he told Hobb. 'I don't want no more trouble before those wagons hit town.'

'I'm sorry, Ma,' Johnny sobbed, burying his face in his mother's skirts. 'I had to do it! I had to! He was going to hurt you!'

As they marched Rachel and her son down the deserted main street, with Emmett limping behind, a bloodied bandanna around his calf, there was only Shona and her girls to watch the strange little procession. She turned to Danielle and Lucy and said, 'We better get ready. This is going to blow up any minute now.'

In the jailhouse, Emmett slumped down on a chair, moaning. Creelock told him to drop his pants.

'Not in front of her,' Emmett objected, pointing at Rachel.

Hobb grinned. 'Hell, Emmett, you was eager to drop them in front of the lady before the boy shot you.'

'It ain't funny, Hobb. You wait till you get shot by some runt of a kid. It ain't funny.'

LaVey was sitting by the fire, amused by such goings-on. Creelock told him to get Mrs Norton and her boy up in one of the cells. After they'd gone Emmett consented to an examination.

'It went right through,' Hobb told

him. He poured whiskey over the ragged wound and chuckled at Emmett's agonized howl. 'Pity the doctor is up at the mine. He could get you all stitched up. All we can do is bandage it and see if you make it to a doctor before gangrene sets in. If you don't, then my guess is you're gonna lose that leg.'

'Everything happens to me,' Emmett complained, almost in tears. 'Shot by some snot-nosed kid and now I'll likely be a cripple. It ain't fair!'

'Hobb is just blowing smoke,' Creelock said. 'Your leg will be fine.'

Even as he reassured Emmett, his blood-red eye fixed Hobb with a hard, purposeful look. Hobb nodded, understanding that once they were done in Lazarus, they'd be riding out without Emmett. And they wouldn't be leaving him alive. It was all right by Hobb, who had never cottoned to men who molested decent women.

★ ★ ★

Rachel insisted she wouldn't share a cell with a drunk smelling of whiskey. 'I got my boy to consider,' she said.

LaVey shrugged, 'It makes no never mind to me, lady. You can go in with the marshal.'

He locked the cell door on them and departed, leaving Raine close by in his chair. Rachel told Holly what had happened as Johnny sat gently sobbing, his arms around his mother.

'I was right to shoot him, weren't I, Marshal?' he asked once he'd settled down some. 'Like you was right to shoot those men on the mountain? He was planning on hurting Ma.'

Holly took the boy's shoulders and looked him in the eye. He said, 'You did right, Johnny. You defended your mother and you got cause to be proud of that.'

Creelock came up a few minutes later, Emmett hobbling painfully behind him. The second he laid eyes on Holly, he pulled his pistol and approached the cell, sticking the gun barrel through the bars.

'No one's left in town to interfere,' he said. 'I want to kill him now.'

Creelock pushed his gun arm aside. 'You'll not do murder in front of the boy,' he snapped. 'We'll deal with Holly before we ride out, away from Mrs Norton and her son.' He turned to address Rachel. 'I assure you no further harm will come to you. Once we're safely away your husband will let you out of there, when he returns. Emmett, since you're no use out on the street you'll stand guard here in place of Raine.' He seized Emmett by the throat. 'And you won't be bothering Mrs Norton any further, you understand?'

Emmett croaked out an agreement and Creelock let him go. As Creelock and Raine went downstairs, Emmett took the vacant chair, wincing as he sat and stretched out the wounded leg.

Holly gave some thought to Creelock's strange chivalry. He could massacre Paiute women and children, but was sensitive to young Johnny not seeing murder done. Of course, once again, Johnny was white.

He gave it a few minutes after Creelock's departure before whispering to Rachel, 'I don't want to endanger you or Johnny any more than I have to, but I got to get out of here. Sam Sugar and his men are riding into an ambush.'

'I know it,' Rachel replied. 'I heard you telling Harvey what's been planned. I might have a way for you to take Emmett.' She eased her son away, motioning for him to stay silent. Johnny nodded without understanding what his mother intended, until she reached into her skirt pockets and produced his catapult, and then his eyes lit up.

'That's why I insisted on sharing this cell,' she said. 'Johnny, you still got some stones in your pocket if I'm not mistaken.'

Holly smiled in respect of her ingenuity and nerve. 'Only trouble is, I can't get a shot at him from in here.'

'I think I can get you a better target,' she said, before going over to the cell door.

'What are you all whispering about in

there?' Emmett shouted. 'I don't like you whispering so you better stop. You got things to say I want to hear them.'

'We were talking about you, Emmett,' Rachel taunted. 'About how I had nothing to worry about back in the storeroom; you ain't man enough to cause me any worry.'

There was silence for few seconds. The barb had struck home. Then Emmett snorted, 'If that brat hadn't gone and shot me, I'd have showed you what a real man is like.'

'Why don't you show me now?'

'You know the captain ordered me to leave you be.'

'Maybe I won't tell him. Maybe you can satisfy me enough that I won't want to tell him. You think you're man enough for that, or are you all talk, Emmett? The other womenfolk all say you got water between your legs. Maybe they're right.'

Holly was staring at Rachel with an almost comical astonishment on his face. It was a whole different side of the prim and correct woman he'd brought to Logan all those weeks ago. He heard the chair creak as Emmett heaved his bulk off it. Rachel's idea had a chance after all. Holly slipped one of the larger stones Johnny had produced into the catapult.

As Emmett hobbled over to the cell door, Rachel stepped back a pace, placing herself between Emmett and the marshal. She had seen Holly do the same up on the mountain, using one of the outlaws to block the hidden shooter's line of sight. Emmett ducked his head around her, but Holly was sitting on the bunk, all of eight feet away.

'So what are you going to do, Emmett?' Rachel asked. Stepping in front of him once more, she began to unbutton her blouse, her eyes boldly holding his.

'You're just joshing with me,' Emmett said sulkily. 'You fought me good in that storeroom. You ain't changed your mind now.'

'You'll never know if you don't unlock that cell door,' Rachel said. 'You've wanted me since you hit town; I've seen it in your eyes.'

'That's true enough. You're a fine-looking woman.'

'But my son can't see what we do. You can lock him and the marshal in here and we'll go in that other room over there. Your friends are going to be busy for some time.'

Holly could see the doubt in Emmett's eyes. He didn't believe her, but even the chance of this woman was too much for him to pass up. He drew his sidearm and unlocked the cell door, holding it wide. 'You stay sat where you are, Marshal,' he said, stepping back to allow Rachel out.

She was between Emmett and the marshal and she judged it just right. At Holly's urgent 'Now!' she dropped to the floor.

Holly loosed his missile and the stone shot straight and true, thudding into Emmett's skull just above his right eye.

He staggered backwards, away from the impact, trying to see through the sudden curtain of blood that fell across his vision. Holly was on him before he could get his senses back, slamming both big, iron-hard fists into his face. The second blow shattered the nose, driving it up into his skull. Emmett dropped beside Rachel like tossed away rags, empty of all life.

'You killed him,' she gasped, the speed and ferocity of Holly's assault leaving her shaken.

Holly took the dead man's pistol. 'I'm sorry all over again, Mrs Norton. This is the second time I've subjected you and the boy to killings.'

Rachel touched his arm with gentle fingers. 'I killed him too, and not so direct as you did. Go and save the town, Nathan Holly. I'll get Johnny out of here.'

Holly nodded his thanks and crept as quietly as possible down the stairs. Creelock was standing over by the half-opened door, ready to greet Sam

Sugar and his deputies when they brought the wagons in. He'd be setting them up for his regulators, who were, without a doubt, all concealed in well chosen firing positions around the main street. Sugar and his men would be caught in a murderous crossfire. Slipping into the back room beyond the office, Holly found the armoury. His own guns were there. He buckled on the gun-belt and checked the loads on both pistols.

So intent was he in watching the street that Creelock never heard the marshal's advance, not until a gun barrel pushed through the fall of white hair and pressed hard against his skull.

'It's over, Creelock. Step out into the street and call to your men to show themselves.'

With only a momentary pause, Creelock did as he was told. One by one the regulators appeared from hiding: Raine from behind the first-floor sign over the Silver Palace; Hobb from an alley across the street; Lamar

LaVey from the wagon-bed he'd been lying in just a few paces away. Three regulators, plus Creelock himself — they were all in the bag, Holly thought. But he was wrong.

Zach Ponder stepped around the corner between the jailhouse and the unfinished church, taking a bead with his rifle. A strengthening wind lifted his coat-tails behind him. It blew in from the north and swung the still lit lantern over the church doorway in short groaning arcs.

Ponder's voice was a low growl as he said, 'Drop the gun or I'll blow all kind of holes in you.'

The moment Holly's Colt hit the boardwalk Creelock stepped away from him and drew his sabre. He laid the point against the marshal's chest. There was relief in his voice as he addressed his subordinate. 'Ponder, I figured you'd be joining us sooner, but I'm right happy you turned up now.'

'They was on to me, Captain. That store feller, he come riding in yelling all

about the dynamite and getting everyone out of the mine. They found where
I'd planted the charges. I had to get the
hell out, just ahead of a lynch mob.'

'But we heard the blasts down here,'
LaVey protested as he clambered over
the wagon's tailgate.

'Well, I reckon that was my idea,'
Holly admitted. 'They blew the charges
away from the mine and sent a rider to
clear the town. I needed all the citizens
out of harm's way in case this got
bloody.'

Creelock gave him an evil grin. 'Well,
you were right about that, Marshal.
This is going to get bloody, and the first
blood spilled is going to be yours. Sugar
and his deputies will be along any time
now, so I can't risk shooting you. Taking
your head off will do the job just as
well.' He raised the sabre above his
head, preparing for the killing stroke.

14

Resurrection

Creelock's sabre flashed as it began its murderous sweep towards Holly's neck.

A window of the jailhouse, near the south corner where Ponder stood, shattered as a chair was shoved through it. The black man swung towards it, bringing his rifle round. In the same moment Holly leapt backwards, clear of the sabre stroke. Pulling the Navy revolver he put two slugs into Ponder's massive frame. The giant swayed but didn't go down. Holly yelled, 'Rachel, get away from the window!'

Ponder loosed several shots through the shattered jailhouse window. Holly hammered the big Navy revolver with lightning speed, emptying it into the black man, the last slug hitting below the chin and ripping his throat away.

'Rachel? Are you all right in there?' Holly yelled.

There was no reply and no time for Holly to check. The sudden explosion of violence had shocked the other regulators into immobility, but for moments only.

Wood splintered around Holly as bullets drummed against the jailhouse wall. He heard a thud of impact as he spun around and saw LaVey staggering forwards, a long feathered shaft sticking out of his lower back. A second arrow joined it a moment later, thudding home between his shoulder blades. Holly had just time enough to spot Tukwa on the roof of the unfinished bank building before Creelock came at him. Raine, over on the first floor balcony of the Silver Palace, saw Tukwa in the same instant.

Holly shouted a warning as Raine turned his aim from Holly to the Paiute, but then his attention was fully on the threat posed by Creelock's sabre.

192

Creelock's action effectively blocked Hobb's view of Holly from the alleyway opposite, just as he'd been about to shoot. The marshal waited until the last second, the Navy revolver empty in his hand. He knew a little about sabre fighting; the further away the fulcrum of the cut was from the point of the sword, the larger the motion needed to execute it. Creelock held the sabre high, at full arm's length; the power from his shoulder when he swept it down would be considerable, but paid for by a complete dedication to the action; it would be hard to change the method of attack once committed to it.

As the sabre began its lethal, downward swing, Holly leapt forwards, not away, ducking under the sabre's sweeping arc and hitting his opponent's midriff with his shoulder. He allowed Creelock's forward momentum to take him up and over his back. Straightening suddenly, he lifted Creelock clear off his feet and threw him to the ground. He hit the boardwalk hard behind Holly, the breath whooshing out of him.

Rifle shots echoed around the town. Raine was firing at Tukwa, raising clouds of stone dust mixed with snow from all around the Paiute's position. Holly expected him to take a hit any second. He was aware that he himself was exposed now that Creelock was on the ground, but then he saw Hobb backing into the street. He was firing towards the alley he'd just vacated. Danielle and Lucy were at the far end of the alley, firing back at him with rifles. He staggered, clearly hit, and slumped down behind a water trough, seeking cover from the murderous fusillade of bullets laid down by Shona's girls.

Holly grinned at the sight. 'Well done, Shona,' he said, 'you pick your girls well.'

Swinging back to Creelock, he found the captain already under attack. An arrow thudded into his left hand as he tried to push upwards from the board-walk. Creelock screamed and Holly turned towards the unfinished bank building. Tukwa was notching another arrow, but Raine, over on the balcony of the Silver Palace, was now taking his time and not shooting wildly. He drew a careful bead on his target and this time he wouldn't miss.

With one gun empty and the other lying several feet away, Holly could only shout a warning, but to no avail: the Paiute was too intent on killing his hated enemy to be distracted, even by his own imminent death.

Raine was about to drop the hammer on Tukwa when Shona stepped on to the boardwalk directly under his position, carrying a shotgun. She raised the Greener and loosed both barrels. The balcony floor exploded upwards, shards and splinters of wood all mixed in with blood and shredded flesh. What was left of Walt Raine crashed down through the shattered balcony floor, landing just feet away from Shona. Smoke from the twin barrels blew wildly on the rising wind like departing spirits.

By the time Holly turned once more to deal with Creelock the man was gone, running towards the church. The broken off arrow lay covered in gore on the boardwalk. Holly reclaimed his Colt from where it lay and sent two bullets after the fleeing man, but Creelock reached the church and went barrelling through the open space that still waited for someone to put a door there. The lantern shattered under a bullet and burning oil spilled across the front of the building. Creelock's clothing took a splattering of oil and Holly saw him beating the flames out as he vanished inside.

Holly was about to follow when he saw Tukwa in pursuit.

'All right,' the marshal said, 'I reckon he's all yours, my friend.'

The gun battle between Hobb and the girls was still proceeding, but the water trough was proving a poor choice of cover. It was disintegrating fast under the fusillade from two rifles. When Holly stepped up behind him and requested him to give up his weapon, Hobb seemed right happy to consent.

'All right, ladies,' Holly called out. 'He's had enough. Fun time's over.'

To Holly's intense relief, Rachel Norton appeared in the doorway of the jailhouse, her son peering out from behind her. Both were shaken, but unharmed.

'I am truly thankful to you, ma'am,' Holly said. 'If you hadn't broke the window Creelock might have got me with that big sticker of his.'

Shona, Danielle and Lucy stepped into the street just as two wagons rolled into sight. Passing the now burning church front, Sam Sugar gave it a mildly interested look, before his world-weary gaze swept across the rest of the carnage. He was driving the lead wagon with a deputy beside him riding shotgun, another deputy was bringing in the second wagon with Tom Loomis up beside him, and two more deputies were riding alongside.

On reining in the horses beside

Holly, Sugar sighed deeply and said, 'Is any town safe from you, Nathan?' He pulled a folded paper from his pocket. Handing it to Holly he stared at all the bodies lying around, thinking he might recognize one particular face. 'Nope, I don't see him nowhere among all these dead men. Has any of this ruckus got to do with the feller on that there dodger? I just got word before leaving Logan that he was seen heading up this way a couple of days ago.'

Coming over to join them, Shona said, 'We got them all.' But Holly shook his head as he looked at the Wanted poster.

'Not yet we don't.'

★　★　★

The skeletal frame of the church was burning fast, the flames funnelled through the building from the two gaping holes where doors should be. Creelock's hoped-for exit out through the back was closed to him not by solid wood, but by something that might prove a lot more immovable. Amongst the heaped piles of rough wood waiting to be turned into more walls and doors and a bell tower, a still and silent figure stood. Beside him, a huge bronze bell waited to be raised.

Creelock growled, 'You git the hell out of my way, you heathen Indian scum, or I'll carve you into little Paiute steaks.' He had a bandanna hastily wrapped around the wounded left hand he was clutching to his chest, but it wasn't tight enough to stop blood seeping through and mixing with the lamp oil on his clothing.

In the flickering firelight Tukwa's face was carved into lines of merciless intent, savage cruelty glittering deep in the darkness of his eyes. He threw the bow aside and shrugged the quiver from his shoulders, dropping the sheepskin coat alongside it. Then he deliberately pulled the tomahawk from his sash and placed himself before the rear doorway, and Creelock's only possible exit.

'You killed my family,' he said. 'My wife, my sons, they cry out for blood. This day they shall have it.'

Creelock looked into the Paiute's black eyes and saw the death he had run from for so long. He had known this day would come. He had been warned many times of a Paiute warrior searching for him; one who had scouted for the army and whose family had all died by Creelock's hand. He had known the moment he saw Tukwa's cavalry trousers that he was the one.

'My sabre against that little hatchet,' he snarled, throwing off the greatcoat. 'You untrained and undisciplined savage, you ain't got a chance in hell of taking me.' But he didn't believe it. The Paiute was consumed by hate, and in Creelock's experience such men didn't die easy.

A gust of wind sent flames leaping around wooden beams that held the ceiling aloft. Even with the cold and snow, the building wouldn't last more than a few minutes. Hearing the cracking of timbers and the angry hiss of flames licking at his back, Creelock advanced on the motionless Paiute.

Tukwa didn't move; he just watched his enemy come to him. When he was just feet away, Creelock snapped to attention, his wounded left hand held tight against his thigh as his right hand raised the sabre above his head with elbow bent. 'On guard then,' he said. 'Let the dance of death begin, no quarter given.'

Tukwa leapt forwards, tomahawk swinging towards Creelock's head. The sabre flashed down, easily deflecting the blow and almost taking the weapon from Tukwa's hand. The Paiute jumped back, out of range of the sabre as Tukwa realized his immediate danger from a counter-strike.

Creelock grinned mirthlessly as he flexed his right wrist. The pivot points with a sabre are wrist and elbow, greatly increasing the rotation of the weapon in any movement. As he stepped towards Tukwa the sabre described glittering arcs and sweeping slash-cuts with a minimal expenditure of effort. Firelight danced along the blade as it scattered falling sparks from the burning timbers above.

Tukwa knew he couldn't get past the reach of the blade and he backed away as Creelock advanced on him. He almost made it under Creelock's guard once, and Creelock reminded himself not to underestimate his adversary. The cavalryman had the skill and reach, but the Paiute had cunning, wiry strength and catlike speed, and a brutal determination to kill.

Creelock paused in his attack, tiring of this game of chasing his prey. Better to allow the enemy to come to him, and the Paiute wanted him very badly. He adopted a low guard position; the wounded hand on his hip and the sabre held with elbow bent, in line with the navel. Then he waited.

Tukwa attacked once more and Creelock effortlessly parried the blow with the side of his blade, and then turned the parry into an attempted belly thrust. Tukwa jumped back from the cut in time to take only a minor wound. The coarse material of his shirt ripped away and a fine line of blood showed across his stomach.

Creelock rasped out a contemptuous, 'First blood,' before moving into the high, or hanging, guard; arm outstretched and sword facing downwards, the curve of the blade towards the swordsman. His left arm was held behind his back as he suddenly danced forwards, the blade flashing in his hand, glittering as red as his damaged eye in the firelight.

Tukwa backed away from the blade, edging around the massive church bell. Creelock followed. Both men were unaware of a blazing beam falling across the front doorway. A sweep of the sabre that would have severed Tukwa's head from his shoulders was stopped at the last instant by the tomahawk catching it and trapping it between the blade and the haft. Tukwa tried to lock it in place as he reached for his hunting knife. Even a second free of the sabre's deadly reach might allow him to take his enemy with the knife.

Seeing the danger posed by the knife, and with his left hand useless, Creelock quickly took advantage of the Paiute's proximity to the huge bronze bell. He closed the gap between them and thrust his entire upper body hard against his opponent, pressing both sabre and tomahawk down against Tukwa's throat and pushing him back against the bell. Tukwa, with the captain's torso pressing him down, had his knife hand effectively trapped between them.

Creelock slammed the sabre's knuckle guard up against Tukwa's jaw. Blood dribbled from the Paiute's mouth and Creelock repeated the blow twice more before heaving himself free of his dazed opponent. He paused for one more powerfully delivered blow, before stepping away.

Blood gushed from the Paiute's mouth and mangled lips. He appeared half-conscious and choking on his own blood. Satisfied that he presented no immediate threat, Creelock raised the sabre high above his head, committing himself to the same high shoulder cut he'd attempted with the marshal. He realized his mistake too late to change his attack to any possible defence.

Tukwa's arm was a blur of motion. He released the tomahawk and it spun across the short space between the two men, embedding itself in Creelock's chest with a dull and fatal thud.

Creelock lurched backwards under the impact. Staring down at the tomahawk, deeply wedged in his upper torso, he dropped the sabre and curled both hands around the haft of the hatchet. He had no strength to try pulling the blade free. His body was already busy with dying, but his mind was still alive to the horror of what had been done to him.

Blood filling both his eyes, not just the one, he lifted his head in a feral cry of agony and terror and saw the section of the roof above him start to give. As Tukwa leapt away from the bell, a rain of burning wood chips fell from the ceiling, covering Creelock's still oil-wet clothing and setting it alight. In moments he was engulfed, his clothing erupting so fiercely it seemed he wore a fiery shroud. He stood there a moment more, wreathed in hellfire, before the crashing ceiling drowned his final screams.

Tukwa turned away and left the inferno behind.

* * *

In the deserted saloon only one man sat waiting. He was at a table near the back, where the gambler had sat that first evening. His face was in shadow, but Holly knew him.

'Jack Weaver,' he said. 'You're the last of them.'

McQueen leaned forward. His mouth bore the fatalistic smile of one who already counts himself among the dead.

Both hands were hidden under the table. 'You finally worked it out,' he said.

'I was sure of it only a moment ago, when Sam Sugar showed me a wanted dodger on the gambler, Nevins. He killed a judge in Virginia City, over a suspect hand of cards. He was on the run and desperate. When he found out who I was, he thought I'd come for him, so he tried to bushwhack me coming back from the mine. He couldn't be the man who murdered my brother in Stillwater. He was too busy killing a judge someplace else.'

'I didn't kill your brother.' McQueen coughed loudly and brought his left hand up, covering his mouth with a handkerchief. The right hand stayed where it was.

Holly ignored the protest of innocence. 'That blood we found on the rocks outside of Stillwater was yours. They told me one of the gang had been shot. I reckon it was pretty bad to alter your appearance so much.'

'It did some damage, maybe to my liver; so the nuns told me anyway. I spent some time being nursed in a convent after we all split up. That's why I was delayed getting here. It took some weight off, left me frail and coughing up blood now and then, and it turned my skin grey. For the rest, I shaved my head and started on growing a beard. I figured someone would be coming after me, figured it would most likely be the marshal's notorious brother. If we'd gotten away with the money I'd have found me a real good doctor to fix me up, in one of them big hospitals back East.'

'You're a murderer, McQueen — or whatever the hell your name really is. You and Tom Loomis were in this together. You knew each other back in New York. He told you about the difficulties the Lazarus Mining Company was having in moving large amounts of money, and you both planned this whole thing.

'You and Loomis arranged for those

drifters to cause trouble in town, so you'd have an excuse for hiring Creelock. You couldn't know how many deputies Sam Sugar might employ to guard the money wagons, and you needed the town buttoned down in case others bought into the fight. You robbed the bank in Stillwater to pay for Creelock's regulators, to make sure they were in your employ more than in Lester Ryle's. You needed Creelock, but you couldn't be sure of him, could you? He had his own men and he might double-cross you. That's why you were bringing in gunhands of your own, to even the odds if it went that way. I guess I messed with your plans by killing them all before they even got here.'

'When Creelock's men were finished with the deputies, we would have finished them. Creelock wouldn't have known I had my own men positioned around town.'

'That's why you were so shocked on hearing I'd killed them all. And when you first laid eyes on me, it wasn't just surprise at opening the door to a stranger; you saw my likeness to my brother, James. You killed Edgar Pullman as well, when he discovered the missing stores of explosives. My guess is he maybe overheard you and Loomis, or maybe Ponder. He didn't know whom to trust and so he just lit out.'

McQueen coughed, raising the handkerchief to his mouth again. The right hand still stayed hidden. 'He was heading down to Logan when Creelock's men caught up to him. But like I said, I didn't kill your brother.'

'I know you didn't,' Holly said. 'Now, do you want to stand up and come along with me, or are you going to use the gun you got pointed at me from under there?'

'I wish I didn't have to.'

'You don't. You can give it up now.'

'How long do you think I'd live in prison?'

'Longer than if you try to take me,' Holly told him.

McQueen kicked the table aside and jumped to his feet with his pistol spitting fire. Holly threw himself to the floor. He hit the ground shooting and saw his slugs take McQueen's legs from under him.

'Give it up!' Holly said, as McQueen lay gasping in pain.

They lay facing one another, Holly with his Colt cocked and ready, McQueen with his back to the wall, his legs holed and bleeding.

'You ain't going far on those,' Holly told him.

'I got this far with a shot-up liver,' McQueen gasped. 'But I guess I ain't going no further.' He raised his pistol.

'You crazy fool! Don't do it!' But Holly knew he wouldn't stop. Having no choice, he exerted the lightest of pressure on the trigger, no more than a lover's gentle caress. The hammer dropped and the gun spat fire and thunder while Holly's big hand absorbed the recoil. A ragged hole opened between McQueen's eyes and his head slapped back against the wall, splattering the fancy wallpaper with bright blood and brain matter.

'Sorry about the cherubs,' Holly said, as he got to his feet. When he heard another gun being cocked behind him he didn't even bother turning around. He knew who it was.

'You figure on shooting me, Catherine, like you did my brother?'

'You know who I am?'

Holly turned and looked at her; saw the hair like spun gold and the eyes like precious gems. 'The face of an angel, James wrote me, and with a nature close to my own. I guess he meant he could see the devil in you, as he always could in me. Sarah Fennell told me you were a lady with hidden depths, but neither she nor James knew the ruthless nature that was really hid away in there. You fell in love with Jack Weaver and you got him free by killing your husband. There was no gun smuggled into the jailhouse and passed to Weaver. You brought it and you used it. The house was set alight to hide your identity and you changed into travelling clothes up on those rocks. The blood on the clothing we found was either from James or McQueen here.

'You know, I been searching for one last man — I never figured on the last killer being a woman. I had some suspicions when I laid eyes on you up at the mine — James described you well. And that remark you made — 'We have to be careful' — you weren't talking about minding the steps.'

Catherine Holly's beautiful eyes were as cold as winter snow when she said, 'You got it all worked out correct, brother-in-law. But now I guess I have to send you to meet up with James, and you can tell him I was sorry I had to kill him, but he got between me and what I wanted.' Her finger was tightening on the trigger when her expression froze as cold as her eyes and her body went rigid. She slowly lowered the gun.

'I'd be happier if you just uncocked it and dropped it entirely,' Shona told her, pressing the Greener even more firmly into her lower back.

The pistol hit the floor just as Sam Sugar led a handcuffed Tom Loomis into the saloon.

★ ★ ★

Holly was all packed and ready to go when Lester Ryle cornered him in the livery stables and grabbed his hand, pumping it enthusiastically and without any let-up for several minutes.

'That's my gun hand, Mr Ryle; I just might be needing it again some time.'

'Well, I just have to thank you, sir, for the service you have done me and this town. Lazarus won't forget you. I'm right sorry you're leaving us, but if you ever want to settle somewhere, remember that you've always got a home here.'

'I'll remember,' Holly promised.

Once Ryle had departed, after another round of profuse thanks, Holly looked up at Tukwa. The Paiute was already mounted and ready to ride.

'Where are you headed?' Holly asked.

'My family are avenged, my shame is washed clean,' Tukwa said. 'Their murderer has paid with his blood, and now I can return to my people. But what of you, Holly; how can you allow the killer of your brother to live one more day? I do not understand this.'

Holly sighed. 'I'm a lawman, Tukwa, not some vigilante killer, no matter how great the urge to do it. Catherine will either hang or more likely spend the rest of her life in a state penitentiary. I doubt that she'll survive it, and if she does she'll be a broken old lady when she next sees the light of day, of no possible harm to anyone. That'll be justice enough for James I guess, and he wouldn't have wanted me to just gun her down. He always held I was too prone to violence, so I figure it'll please him. I'll find out when I see him again.'

Tukwa took his leave with as much emotion as the Paiute could ever show, which was pretty much none. Holly grinned to himself as he rode down the main street. He'd miss the Paiute's company on the trail; he didn't talk much and such companionable silence could be restful. Harvey and Rachel Norton were standing outside their store, talking with the reverend.

'Sorry about the church,' Holly said, eyeing the charred remains.

'It will be rebuilt,' Ellis assured him.

Holly nodded. 'I guess it will. Resurrection is what this town is all about.' He looked at Rachel Norton and nodded his thanks. 'I owe you, ma'am. If you hadn't broke that window just when you did — '

Rachel Norton shocked him by standing on tiptoe and kissing his cheek. Harvey laughed at his embarrassment and all Holly could think of to say was, 'Well, all right then. You all take care.'

'Where are you heading, Holly?' Rachel asked.

'It'll be Christmas soon,' he replied, 'and I reckon on spending it with my sister and her family. As you once told me, ma'am, family are important and shouldn't become strangers.'

As he trotted on down the street to the Silver Palace he admitted that Rachel Norton was a lady full of surprises.

Shona was his last goodbye before riding out, and it caused him the most unease. He always hated taking his leave of Shona Gordillo, but he always did it anyway. That they'd meet up again somewhere, in some new cow town or boom town of whatever persuasion, he didn't doubt.

He spent an hour with her and then he rode out with her voice still calling after him.

'You remember, Nathan Holly, when you get that first million you come and find me. I hold you to it, you big buffalo.'

Shona smiled to herself. Someday, she told herself, with or without that million, she had serious plans for Nathan Holly.

She watched him ride into the haze of a low winter sun. He was soon out of sight.

We do hope that you have enjoyed reading this large print book.

Did you know that all of our titles are available for purchase?

We publish a wide range of high quality large print books including:
Romances, Mysteries, Classics
General Fiction
Non Fiction and Westerns

Special interest titles available in large print are:
The Little Oxford Dictionary
Music Book, Song Book
Hymn Book, Service Book

Also available from us courtesy of Oxford University Press:
Young Readers' Dictionary
(large print edition)
Young Readers' Thesaurus
(large print edition)

For further information or a free brochure, please contact us at:
Ulverscroft Large Print Books Ltd.,
The Green, Bradgate Road, Anstey,
Leicester, LE7 7FU, England.
Tel: (00 44) **0116 236 4325**
Fax: (00 44) **0116 234 0205**